A DROP OF HOPE

Keith Calabrese

SCHOLASTIC INC.

With special thanks to

Amla Sanghvi

ISBN 978-1-338-54103-8

10 9 8 7 6 5 4 3 2 1   19 20 21 22 23

Printed in the U.S.A.   40
First printing 2019
Book design by Baily Crawford

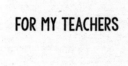
FOR MY TEACHERS

This story starts with a wish and ends in a crime.

The wish isn't granted, and the crime is never punished.

Life is like that sometimes.

But that isn't always a bad thing . . .

1

A SURPRISE IN THE ATTIC

Ernest Wilmette was alone in his dead grandfather's house, and he really wished he wasn't.

He stood in front of the attic door. It was thinner than a usual door, and shorter, too. Probably by about six to eight inches. Not that it would make any difference to Ernest. Ernest was eleven, twelve in four months. He'd started sixth grade—middle school—a month ago, but you wouldn't guess it to look at him. He still had to sit in the back seat of the car because he wasn't tall or heavy enough for the air bag.

Small or not, Ernest had made a promise. Not only that, he'd made it to a dying man. Ernest suspected those were the kinds of promises you really had to keep.

It had been late last spring. They were in Grandpa Eddie's kitchen, just the two of them, making sandwiches.

"Ernest, can you do something for me?" Grandpa Eddie had said.

"Sure," Ernest said, expecting his grandfather to send him to the fridge to fetch some mustard.

"After I'm gone, promise me that you'll clean out my attic. Okay?"

It was a strangely serious request. Stranger still for Ernest, who didn't know how sick his grandfather really was. No one ever talked about it around Ernest. Small Ernest. Too small for the truth.

He was scared to ask the obvious question, but too curious not to at the same time. "What's up in the attic?"

Grandpa Eddie gazed down at Ernest, a knowing, weary look in his eyes. "Oh, just some things I should have parted with a long time ago," he said in a distant, almost spooky voice that Ernest hoped was just the medication. His parents had told him that much, at least. That the pills Grandpa Eddie was taking might make him a little woozy and confused. Even still, Ernest couldn't help but notice how his grandfather had been looking at him these past few weeks, as if he knew some secret about Ernest but wouldn't say what it was.

"Okay," Ernest said, uncertainly.

"Good," the frail old man said, just as suddenly back to himself again. He patted Ernest on the top of the head. "Now that's sorted, let's have some lunch."

Ernest didn't know how to explain what happened. There was a brief moment of quiet, and then Grandpa Eddie simply walked over to the fridge to get them a drink. But something about that brief moment seemed significant, the way some moments just weigh more than others. And something about the way they then quietly, almost reverently, ate their turkey sandwiches at the kitchen table suggested to Ernest that he and his grandfather had just sealed a fateful pact, like the blood oaths the Greek gods were always making in the books Ernest loved to read.

Shortly after that, Grandpa Eddie took a bad turn. He grew feverish and weak. He coughed up blood and had to move into the hospital. The doctors put a tube in his arm that pumped medicine into his veins. It made him drowsy and confused.

The last time Ernest saw him, Grandpa Eddie was really thin, and his skin was gray and loose on his bones. The dying man was awake, and pleading in a panicked, rasping voice.

"Tell Ernest! Tell him he can't forget the attic!" Grandpa Eddie sat up in his bed, something he hadn't done for weeks. He looked right at Ernest, but with no recognition in his eyes.

"It's just the drugs, honey," Ernest's mom said soothingly as his dad tried to calm Grandpa Eddie down. "He doesn't know what he's saying."

Grandpa Eddie collapsed back onto his bed. He was whimpering now, and when he spoke next he sounded like a child. "I kept them," his grandfather said, his voice sounding faint and far away. "I kept them all." Grandpa Eddie, looking both scared and relieved, reached up to the ceiling.

"Rollo," the old man said. "I kept them."

And then he died.

That was eight weeks ago.

Ernest really wanted to leave, to go back down the steps, out the front door, and forget about the whole thing. That dark and dusty attic had been creepy enough even when his grandfather was alive. But he couldn't back out now; he just couldn't. He'd promised.

He closed his eyes, took a breath, and opened the door.

The attic was a mess. There was junk everywhere, and it took Ernest a good twenty minutes to clear a path down the center of the room.

He moved a tower of boxes from the far wall, revealing one of the eyebrow dormer windows. Unblocking the window gave the attic a much-needed infusion of sunlight.

In the corner of the room, Ernest saw an old rocking chair with a plastic-wrapped patchwork quilt draped over the back. On the seat of the rocking chair sat a carefully arranged pile of boxes.

Stepping closer, he could see that the boxes contained toys— old toys, but new at the same time. They were old in that they'd been there for a long while, but new in that they were still in their original packaging and had never been opened.

Ernest's first thought was that he'd stumbled upon some early presents that Grandpa Eddie had bought for him before he died. But these boxes were old, antiques even. All of them perfectly preserved: mint, a collector would say. Ernest wasn't sure what or who these toys were for, but they were way too old to have been meant for him.

He was about to move on from the rocking chair to another corner of the room when it happened. A sliver of light from the window broke through and beamed unmistakably, like a spotlight, on the rocking chair full of toys, shining on one box in particular: an art set.

He picked up the box. It was heavier than he'd expected. The case was wood—real, solid wood. Inside were a series of sketch pencils, tubes of paint, brushes, chalk, charcoals, and some drawing tablets. Though a set for beginners, it was serious business nonetheless. Unlike modern disposable art sets, which expect to be trashed and the pieces lost the minute they're opened, this was a set to treasure.

The light from the window made the set glow in a way that

Ernest felt was strangely, irresistibly beckoning. Though it could have simply been a trick of the light, some odd angle of refraction against the dirty glass, Ernest couldn't help but get that heavy-moment feeling again, like when his grandfather had first asked him to clean the attic.

As he held the wooden box delicately in his hands, Ernest remembered the knowing look Grandpa Eddie had given him that day. "Just some things I should have parted with a long time ago," he had said. Now, as Ernest looked down at the art set, it was like fate was giving him an elbow in the ribs and saying, "Go on, take it. You might be needing that."

He stared at the box a little longer, but fate apparently refused to be more specific on the matter.

RYAN HARDY VERSUS THE MACHINE

Piece-of-junk lawn mower.

Ryan Hardy crouched down and stared at the overturned machine. Overturned by him after it had started coughing up freshly cut grass. Again.

It was his own fault. He'd let Mrs. Haemmerle's lawn go for too long, let the grass get too thick. He'd only done about a quarter of the yard so far, and the mower had already backed up on him three times. Because he'd tried to rush it, keeping the mower on the usual, lowest setting even though the grass had grown too heavy for it.

Ryan glared down at the mower, lying belly-up in the grass like it was perfectly content to recline there all afternoon. If it were capable, Ryan was confident the machine would be making a rude gesture at him right about now.

Good deeds may or may not go unpunished, but Ryan Hardy knew one thing for sure: They definitely snowball. Ever since Mr. Haemmerle had died, going on two years now, Ryan had been mowing the old widow's lawn. And shoveling her walk and driveway when it snowed. Then there were the leaves in the fall, rain gutters in the spring, garbage bins out to the curb and back to the side of the house every week. Basically, Ryan did any odd job around that house that might lead to a broken hip or a heart attack if the old lady tried to do it herself. And he did it all for free.

Ryan knew Mrs. Haemmerle was on what adults call a "fixed income," which was a polite way of saying someone didn't have any money. He was no stranger to the little signs of people trying to cut costs. Her house was clean and well kept, but there was never that much food in the kitchen, and all the appliances were really old. She didn't have a computer or a cell phone, and Ryan knew plenty of people who had those things even when they didn't have much else.

It wasn't a hard lawn to take care of, and most days cutting it for free made Ryan feel pretty good.

But today it didn't. Today it made him feel like a chump who was wasting his Sunday.

Ryan looked up from the overturned lawn mower and noticed an expensive, foreign sedan easing down the street. A North Side car.

Ernest Wilmette. He should have guessed. The Wilmettes were rich. They lived in the most expensive house in town. It was one of those modern designs, all glass and hard lines and sharp edges. The kind of house that belonged perched on top of a mountain. But there aren't any mountains in Ohio, so the Wilmettes had to settle for the biggest hill on the North Side.

Mrs. Wilmette was driving and Ernest was sitting in the back seat. He spotted Ryan and waved; obliged, Ryan waved back. He was obliged because his dad was the foreman at the factory that Ernest's dad owned. Obliged because he didn't like Ernest, and didn't want to wave at him.

Ryan had spent all of yesterday afternoon cutting the other Wilmette lawn, the one across the street. He'd been doing that yard since the spring, when Eddie Wilmette, Ernest's grandfather, got sick and then died. Ryan didn't really know Eddie Wilmette very well, but he liked the old man because he let you call him Eddie even if you were a kid. Though rolling in dough, Eddie never moved out of the South Side and had mowed his own lawn until he got too sick to do it anymore. That was when Ernest's dad had hired Ryan to keep up the yard while the family figured out what to do with the now empty house.

Deep down, Ryan knew Ernest wasn't that bad. For a rich kid, he didn't act stuck-up or better than anyone. But the kid was just so clueless and carefree. He was always smiling, always friendly, always in a good mood. One of those "look on the bright side" types, because that's all he'd ever known, the bright side. Nothing ever seemed to bother Ernest.

And that was what bothered Ryan.

BACK SEAT BOY

Ernest's mom was sitting on the porch when he came downstairs.

"Get what you need?" she asked as they headed back to the car.

"I think so," Ernest said.

As they drove down Grandpa Eddie's street, Ernest spied a boy mowing a lawn. It was Ryan Hardy, from Ernest's class.

Ernest didn't want Ryan to see him in the back seat, which meant that Ryan inevitably would. Ernest tried to look away, but it was too late. Ryan spotted him and Ernest knew he had to wave, however lamely, as he sat in the back seat like a baby. Ryan probably never sat in the back seat in his life, not even when he really was a baby. And he'd been mowing lawns since he was seven. Seven! Ernest's mom wouldn't let Ernest mow their lawn because he still had to reach up for the bar.

His mom didn't talk much as they drove across town. If she even noticed the art set on the seat next to him, she didn't say. Ernest knew she had a lot on her mind. His dad had been working all the time lately, even when he was home. His parents were both worried. He wasn't sure about what, exactly, but he could tell.

They never said as much, of course. Like with Grandpa Eddie's illness, they didn't talk about serious things around Ernest, and it bothered him. It was like riding in the back seat in the car, but worse.

It was like he was riding in the back seat of his own family.

MRS. HAEMMERLE

The car passed, and Ryan returned his attention to the mower. He got down on his knees, pulled back the discharge guard, and started to clean the clogged-up trimmings from the mower deck.

"Ryan, dear. Be careful!" The screen door slammed as Mrs. Haemmerle scurried outside, a glass of lemonade in her shaky little hand.

"I'm okay, Mrs. Haemmerle. The engine's off."

"Oh, still," she said anxiously. "I don't know."

Ryan removed his hand from the mower deck and stepped back from the machine.

Mrs. Haemmerle visibly relaxed. "Would you like some lemonade?"

She was a tiny woman. She weighed maybe ninety pounds, wet. After a five-course steak dinner. As she held the glass of lemonade out to Ryan, she looked like she might tip forward from the shift in balance.

"Yes, thank you," Ryan said, taking the glass. Her lemonade was freshly made, no powder, and he knew it must be hard work for her to squeeze all those lemons. The ends of her fingers were visibly bent with arthritis. It probably really hurt, not that she'd complain. Mrs. Haemmerle was the sweetest person Ryan had ever met.

After she went back inside, Ryan readjusted the setting on the mower to do the yard twice, the right way. But he also promised himself that in four years, when he got his driver's license, he'd drive that piece-of-junk lawn mower out to the county reservoir. And throw it in.

2

A WEIRD ENCOUNTER

After raising the blade height on the mower, Ryan finished Mrs. Haemmerle's yard without further frustration. In fact, the second pass—at the regular height—seemed to breeze by.

Mrs. Haemmerle came out the back door, a couple of neatly folded bills in her hand.

"It's covered, Mrs. Haemmerle," he said, waving away the money.

She looked at him, confused as usual. "It is?"

"Yep. We're square. You paid me at the beginning of the month. Remember?"

Mrs. Haemmerle shook her head doubtfully. "Well, if you say so, Ryan."

She put the money in the pocket of her apron as if sensing it didn't really belong there.

"I just have to take the trash out. Unless you need anything else today?"

"No, sweetie," Mrs. Haemmerle said. "Go on. Go play while there's still some daylight left."

Ordinarily, Ryan would not like someone suggesting he "go play," but he knew Mrs. Haemmerle well enough to take her meaning, which was more like "go live, have fun, be young."

"Okay," Ryan said. "I'll come around on Thursday." Thursday was grocery day.

Mrs. Haemmerle thanked Ryan one more time and then, patting the money in her apron pocket as if trying to recall unfinished business, made her way back inside.

Ryan was wheeling the yard bins out to the curb when Lizzy MacComber came out of her house. She was in Ryan's class; he'd known her for about as long as he could remember. They used to play together frequently when they were little, so much so that half the time they would go into each other's houses without knocking.

Not so much anymore.

"Hey, Ryan," she said. She had a stack of magazines in her arms.

"Oh," Ryan said. "Hey."

"Can I ask you a question?" Lizzy smiled, but in a funny way. She had a look in her eye that Ryan couldn't place. Kind of like when someone's setting you up for a joke.

"What?"

Lizzy held up one of the magazines. It was about fashion, the kind his mom would sometimes get. The model on the cover had long blond hair and wore a tight dress with a low neckline.

"Do you think she's pretty?"

It was what they call a loaded question. Of course Ryan thought the model was pretty. That's why they put her on the magazine.

"I don't know." He shrugged.

"What about her?" Lizzy quickly flipped to a dog-eared page from another magazine. This model had short, dark hair and a high skirt that showed a lot of her leg. Ryan really didn't get what Lizzy was playing at, but it was making him uncomfortable.

"I said, I don't know. Why are you asking me?"

"C'mon, Ryan," Lizzy said in that how-can-you-not-be-getting-this way that girls often use with boys. "It's not a hard question. Is she pretty?"

"Sure. Yeah. She's pretty," he blurted, hoping it would end there. "Okay?"

"Prettier than me?"

Ryan scowled. "Stop being weird," he snapped, louder than he'd intended, and walked past her down the sidewalk.

Lizzy stood there, holding the magazines to her chest with a hurt look on her face.

"I was just asking!" Lizzy called after him, but he kept walking.

THE DIFFERENCE A YEAR MAKES

Lizzy threw the magazines down on the couch. Then she threw herself down on the couch and buried her face in the cushion. She'd never felt so stupid in her entire life. Ryan had looked at her like she was gross and absurd. Like she was nuts.

The minute she'd asked him about the first model, she knew it was a mistake. Making big, dopey eyes at Ryan and cocking her head to the side when she talked wasn't going to work on him. And the way she'd talked—all breathy and singsongy—like it wasn't even her voice!

That's because it wasn't her voice, just like those weren't really her magazines. They both belonged to Lizzy's cousin Chelsea.

Chelsea was older than Lizzy and liked to treat her younger cousin like something between a pet and an old doll. Not the kind of doll a girl pampers or cherishes, but rather the kind of doll that's expendable, the off-brand doll she can experiment on and not care if she messes it up.

For the last few months, Lizzy had been spending most of her Saturdays at Chelsea's house while Lizzy's mom was working at the hospital. And recently, Chelsea had decided to make Lizzy her *project*. Chelsea and her mom, Lizzy's aunt Patty, had lengthy conversations, right in front of Lizzy, about how to fix her wardrobe and her hair and her skin and essentially make a new, improved young woman out of her.

Lizzy certainly didn't want to be anyone's project, and she realized that the whole idea was really just a thinly veiled way for her aunt and her cousin to openly pick her apart in the guise of constructive criticism. Lizzy knew what they thought about her and her mom. She saw the way Chelsea and Aunt Patty looked down on her mom when she dropped Lizzy off, wearing her hospital scrubs and no makeup. Lizzy knew what Aunt Patty was thinking at the end of the day, when her mom, worn out from her shift, came to pick up Lizzy and bring her home.

It's so sad, but that's what happens when you can't keep your man.

So yesterday, when Chelsea dropped those fashion magazines in Lizzy's arms, she knew what her cousin was really saying.

Here you go. Better do your homework, unless you want to end up like your mom.

The worst part of it, though, was that sometimes Lizzy feared that her aunt and her cousin might be right. Lizzy loved her mom, but she saw how sad she got when her dad didn't come by like he'd said he would. She'd heard her mom crying in her room afterward. Lizzy didn't want to end up like that. She was scared of ending up like that.

Everything had been so much simpler a year ago. A year ago she'd have gone outside to say hey to Ryan, just like she used to. She and Ryan had been friends since they were little, like diapers-little.

But they weren't little anymore, and a year made a big difference. A year ago Lizzy's dad was still around. A year ago she didn't have to go to Aunt Patty's house every Saturday while her mom pulled a weekend shift at the hospital. A year ago she never would have done anything so stupid as try to flirt with Ryan Hardy using fashion magazines.

Try as she might, Lizzy couldn't stop replaying the horrible encounter over in her mind, the attention to detail that served her so well in school now providing achingly perfect recall of every agonizing moment. It was as if once she started, she couldn't stop herself. After she'd shown him the first picture, she just had to show him the second, and would have shown him more, picture after picture, making a bigger and bigger fool of herself . . .

If Ryan hadn't gotten so annoyed that he'd just turned and walked away from her.

She wanted to be mad at him, but in truth he'd done her a favor. Like the mercy rule in Little League baseball, he'd put her out of her misery.

Lizzy heard her mom stirring in her bedroom and wiped the tears from her eyes.

"Hey, Mom," Lizzy said quickly as the door opened.

"Hey there, sweetie." Lizzy's mom rubbed her eyes. They were puffy, and one side of her face was pink from where it had been smushed into the pillow. "My word, I was really out," she said with a little laugh as she ran her fingers through her bedhead.

Wow, does she look like a wreck. No wonder . . .

Lizzy shut her eyes to block the rest of it out. She hated letting that stuff in her head, hated seeing her mom through her aunt's and cousin's eyes.

Lizzy's mom went into the kitchen and checked the fridge. Unsatisfied, she came back out and looked at Lizzy, closely. Lizzy was afraid her mom would see the red crying splotches on her face.

"You know," her mom said, as if coming to a big decision. "I could just murder a cheeseburger tonight. Whatd'ya say?"

Lizzy didn't really want a burger, but her mom was trying to do something special. Bonding time or whatever.

"Sure," she said. "That sounds great."

WELCOME TO CLIFFS DONNELLY

Ryan came in through the kitchen. He could hear the TV in the den. It was one of his dad's shows. He could tell right away by the sound of men arguing.

His dad had been watching shows like this a lot lately. Men in suits, sitting around a table and yelling at each other. Always, they were yelling. Even when they agreed, they still yelled. They were always angry, these men in their suits—angry at all the people who were ruining everything for the rest of us. Ryan wasn't exactly sure who was doing the ruining and less sure about how they were, in fact, doing it; mostly the men in suits seemed to blame people in other countries or people who lived here but looked like people who came from other countries.

They were the kind of men his dad would have once dismissed—stuffed shirts, he used to call them. Men with tough words but soft hands and pudgy, pink faces. Men who weren't worth listening to.

But now his dad was listening, and Ryan didn't understand why. All those shows did was make his dad angry, too. Sometimes Ryan would pass by the den and overhear his dad muttering back at the TV, growling "What a mess" and "Whole country's going down the toilet" in a dark voice that didn't sound like his own.

And Ryan knew his dad wasn't the only one.

About a mile from Ryan's house, on the side of the road at the edge of town, was a simple white sign with black lettering that was supposed to read, in an official yet friendly font:

WELCOME TO CLIFFS DONNELLY
POPULATION: 22,177

Cliffs Donnelly. It was a strange name for a town, if for no other reason than it begged the question, why not just call it Donnelly Cliffs, or even Cliffs *of* Donnelly? According to one of Ryan's teachers, Mr. Earle, the original name of the town (back when it was first incorporated in 1835) was supposed to be Clifton Donnelly, after the two most prominent families in town, the Cliftons and the Donnellys. But then the Donnelly family decided to bribe the town sign maker into cutting out the Cliftons altogether. Unfortunately, the Donnellys, while devious, weren't all that punctual, and by the time they got around to bribing the sign maker, he'd already carved the first four letters, *Clif,* and thus the town of Cliffs Donnelly was born.

That was what Mr. Earle said, anyway. Though you could never really be sure with him. That man sure knew how to tell a story. Ryan did know one thing for sure, though. There weren't any cliffs in Cliffs Donnelly.

Of course, while Ryan was sure that *Welcome to Cliffs Donnelly* was what it said on the sign at the northern edge of town, here on the South Side someone had taken a can of black spray paint and traced over the *i,* one *f,* the *o,* one *n,* one *l,* and the *y,* so that all you really noticed on the sign was:

if on ly

If only.

It was fast becoming the town's nickname. Because there was always another factory closing down, another business moving away, more people out of work, making the town a bit emptier than it was before.

People on both sides of town were now starting to see Cliffs Donnelly as a place where "if only" had gone from a joke to a lament. People who used to say things like "If only I hadn't blown out my knee in high school I could've gone pro," or "If only I had practiced guitar more I could have been a rock star," were now saying, "If only the factory hadn't shut down I could've kept the house," and "If only I didn't have to choose between health insurance and the gas bill." Of course these people always knew they'd never go pro or be rock stars. But that had always been okay because they also knew that if they worked hard and lived right, things more or less would work out. Only they weren't working out, not anymore.

And it was making people like Ryan's dad angry.

Ryan loved his dad, but lately he didn't like being around him much. Not so long ago they used to hang out a lot. They used to watch TV together all the time. Old movies, mostly. Ryan and his dad hadn't watched a movie together in months.

Ryan went upstairs and found his mom in Declan's room. Declan was asleep in his crib, and his mom was reading one of her books in the rocking chair. She was always reading when she had a spare moment. Or doing a crossword in pen. And she could do the daily Sudoku crazy fast. She was by far the smartest person Ryan knew.

"Too smart for this family," Ryan's dad used to joke. Back when he used to joke.

"Hi, honey," she whispered. "Finished up Mrs. Haemmerle's lawn?"

Ryan nodded. "Finally," he sighed, his body sagging against the doorframe.

"Hungry?" She started to rise.

Ryan waved her off. "I'm good, Mom," he said softly, wanting to leave her to her reading. Soon Declan would be up and then there'd be a whirlwind of dinner, laundry, bath time.

Ryan helped with Declan where he could, but there was no way around it; the kid just didn't like him. Wouldn't let Ryan hold him, wouldn't even let Ryan near him just in case Ryan might try to set him down next to an electrical outlet with a handful of silverware.

Ryan peeked into Declan's crib. His little brother was lying on his back, his arms spread out and his legs splayed open like an overturned frog.

Declan stirred, crinkling his nose in an irritated baby scowl.

Even asleep he doesn't like me, Ryan thought.

By the time Ryan had taken a shower and changed, Declan was awake and his mom was downstairs with him, making dinner.

Ryan came down to help set the table. Then his mom sent him into the den to call his dad to eat.

He found his dad asleep in his chair, a frown on his face as if he could still hear the arguing men on the television. Ryan shook him gently on the shoulder. "Dad? Dad?" he said.

Ryan's dad opened his eyes narrowly.

"Dinner, Dad," Ryan said.

His dad blinked and took a long breath, nodding that he'd be there directly.

It was quiet during dinner, except for Declan, who was still too young to be affected by uncomfortable silence. Ryan's parents filled the spaces with some small talk about the meal, and how Ryan's dad would probably be working late all this week.

That wasn't news, as Ryan's dad had been working late most nights. Though he didn't talk about it much, Wilmette Stamping, Tool & Die was in trouble. For as long as Ryan could remember, factories had been closing down all over the area and relocating to Mexico and Asia. Ryan knew there was talk that the Wilmettes' factory might be the next to go.

"Did you take care of the Wilmette lawn this weekend?" Ryan's dad asked him.

Ryan nodded. "Saturday."

Ryan's dad took a business envelope out of his back pocket and handed it to Ryan. His dad claimed to have no idea how much Ryan had charged his boss, having made Ryan negotiate his fee directly with Mr. Wilmette. "That's between you and Mr. Wilmette," his dad had said. "It's your business."

Ryan's dad was still looking at him after Ryan put the money away. "Did Haemmerle's today, then?"

"Yeah," said Ryan.

"She still not paying you?" he said, asking in that way adults do when they already know the answer.

"It's okay, Dad."

"Doesn't sound okay to me," his dad said, spearing a baby potato with his fork.

"Doug . . ." his mom said softly.

"He can answer, Karen."

Ryan looked directly at his dad, but not too directly. "As you say, it's my business."

Ryan saw the muscles tense in his dad's neck. Parents always tell their kids to stand up for themselves, but they never mean for their kids to do it with *them*. And Ryan was pushing it double by using his dad's words back on him.

Doug Hardy stared at his son for a long moment. Then he slid back his chair. "All right," he said with a dismissive growl as he got up and went back into the den.

WILMETTE STAMPING, TOOL & DIE

Quiet is louder in a big house. And Ernest's house was a big house. Ernest's mom came from a big family and had wanted a big family, too. Both his parents had. So they built a huge house, with a huge yard, the kind meant to be overrun with lots of kids— kids who would yell and play and dirty up the rug.

But there had only been Ernest. Just Ernest. Small Ernest.

After dinner Ernest brought his dad some coffee, like he did most nights. His dad thanked him in a distracted way, absorbed so deeply in his work that Ernest was surprised his father even realized he'd entered the room.

Ernest's dad ran the family business, Wilmette Stamping, Tool & Die. It made, well, pieces.

Every machine, whether it's a toaster or a tractor, an alarm clock or a jumbo jet, a dishwasher or a pacemaker, is made up of a bunch of little parts, little pieces that have to fit and move together perfectly for the machine in question to work. Individually the parts themselves never look like much. Just funny shapes with holes and wedges, curves and angles, nothing to take note of, really.

As long as the machine in question works.

Wilmette Stamping, Tool & Die was established in 1945 by Edgar Wilmette, Ernest's great-grandfather, who had been a machinist and engineer with the Air Force. He was good at making these little pieces. And so was his son, Grandpa Eddie. And so was Ernest's dad, Eric.

So good that Wilmette Stamping, Tool & Die now boasted over two hundred employees on a sprawling industrial center spanning two and a half acres, complete with its own dedicated traffic light for that easy-to-miss turnoff for State Route 41.

After Ernest gave his dad his coffee, he went up to his room. He read some, then got ready for bed and packed his bag for school tomorrow. The art set was sitting on his desk, right where he'd left it after coming home from Grandpa Eddie's, kind of like it was waiting for him. He had a feeling that it was more than just an old, forgotten toy. That maybe it, too, was a piece of something, and that it just needed to be matched with other pieces. New pieces.

And then things would start working again.

3

THE WALL

Rod Serling Middle School was built in the 1930s. Three stories tall, the building was shaped like a giant rectangle, with a large courtyard area in the hollowed center.

Originally, the idea had been to set a row of windows along the perimeter of the courtyard with large glass doors installed at either end, thereby allowing the courtyard to open up as a pass-through. Several decades, two name changes to the school, various budget concerns, bureaucratic squabbles, and one glazier strike later, the notion of such a walk-through courtyard was but a distant memory.

Instead, a dreadful compromise had been reached: The side

near the school entrance had the large glass doors that opened into the courtyard, but the other side did not. Instead, a hideous, concrete, cinder-block wall managed to clash equally well with both the surrounding glass windows and the building's original brickwork.

Young Winston Patil spent every morning looking at that ugly cinder-block wall until the five-minute bell prodded him on to Mr. Earle's class. Winston was the new kid. His family had moved to Cliffs Donnelly over the summer. And every morning before school, as he walked in the front doors, he'd find himself drifting toward the courtyard windows, where he would just stand and stare intently at the barren, concrete eyesore.

And imagine.

MR. EARLE

Mr. Earle was Ryan's favorite teacher. But then, he was a lot of kids' favorite teacher. He was cool the way adults often thought they were but really weren't. He was cool because he didn't try to be. In fact, in a lot of ways, Mr. Earle was really kind of dorky. His dress shirts all had bold, striking patterns, thick stripes or busy plaids, and his chinos were always ridiculous statement colors, like salmon or sky blue. He even had a chartreuse pair.

He was tall and biracial and kids were always asking him where he was from, ethnicity-wise, even though you weren't supposed to do that. Mr. Earle made a game out of it, however, and never claimed the same cultural heritage two times in a row. Some days he said he was Irish Dominican, other days Polish Colombian or Welsh Kenyan or Creole Hawaiian. Ryan suspected these different ancestries were "teachable moments" meant to subtly suggest that they were all Americans, and it shouldn't matter, anyway. Though maybe he was also trying to trick his students into looking at a map or a globe once in a while.

Ryan's sixth-grade class had Mr. Earle for English and homeroom. Not that homeroom was an actual class; it was really just a bookmark in the day, a place to put kids who were either waiting for or had just finished lunch. Most of the time homeroom was a chance to get some homework done or, if your teacher was mellow enough, talk and hang out with friends.

Except on Mondays. Mondays were Council Days.

Council Days were designed for kids to get the chance to air out their opinions on various issues. Teachers were encouraged to give each week a special topic—bullying, peer pressure, stress—but Mr. Earle went for a less direct approach. He knew that if you got kids talking, the rest would take care of itself, but that if you tried to manipulate the conversation, the kids would invariably clam up.

Mr. Earle also had an ace up his sleeve: He could talk. The man was a master storyteller. So whenever the conversation petered out, Mr. Earle always had a story to fill the silence. It didn't matter if it was an old fairy tale or a Greek myth or the plot of a thick Russian novel or something that happened to his crazy roommate in college; Mr. Earle could suck you in and have you hanging on every detail.

"Today," said Mr. Earle, "I thought it would be fun to talk a bit about folklore." He was walking around the room, weaving between the desks. "Who can tell me what folklore is, exactly?"

No one answered. Mr. Earle waited patiently for a moment and then did what they were all waiting for him to do.

Call on Lizzy.

"Okay, Lizzy? Care to help us out?"

Lizzy always knew the answer. "Folklore is the collected myths or stories of a particular area."

"Excellent. Thanks, Lizzy."

Ryan thought about yesterday, when she came over to Mrs. Haemmerle's house with those fashion magazines. It had occurred to him that night, after dinner, that maybe Lizzy was trying to joke around with him.

Maybe she just wanted to hang out like they used to. Before her dad left.

"When we talk about folklore," Mr. Earle continued, "we're talking about legends or fairy tales that have been passed down through generations."

"Like Cinderella," Paige Barnett said. "Or Goldilocks."

"Exactly. Good."

"Or Bigfoot," Jamie Dahl snickered.

"Bigfoot's real!" Aaron Robinette blurted out, bouncing up and down in his seat. He was always bouncing, always restless. It drove their other teachers crazy, but Mr. Earle just ignored it. "Although, personally, I prefer to call the creature Sasquatch."

"Creature? Right. It's a guy. In a suit," Jamie said. Those two were always going at each other.

"Shut up, Jamie!"

"Actually, Bigfoot raises a very interesting point," Mr. Earle calmly cut in. "Often folklore can be a confusing blend of truth and fiction." He was good at that, solving an argument without it looking like he was taking sides. "In fact, one of its main functions was to try to make sense of things people couldn't understand."

"And then find someone to blame for it," Lizzy added.

Mr. Earle perked up. "Yes! Scapegoating. Good, Lizzy. Who here, other than Lizzy, can tell us what a scapegoat is?"

"Someone who takes the blame for something they didn't do," Paige said.

"Right," Mr. Earle said. "Quite a lot of folklore was invented by frightened villagers looking to explain why their crops went bad or their chickens disappeared or people started getting sick. Now, combine that fear with the pre-existing suspicion and xeno-phobia already aimed at gypsies, outsiders, and other itinerant people in the region and voilà—we've just invented witches, werewolves, and vampires."

The class laughed, even though Ryan guessed Lizzy was the only one of them who knew what *xenophobia* and *itinerant* meant. Ryan figured the gist of it, though, was that if you look different from everyone else and bad things start happening, sooner or later you're going to get run out of town for it.

Mr. Earle clapped his hands together in an okay-moving-on kind of way and said, "Can anyone else think of other situations where communities rely on legends and folklore?"

The class got quiet again. Mr. Earle waited for a moment and then offered up an idea.

"How about entertainment? People had to do something before TV, right?"

The class laughed again. Ryan saw Mr. Earle's gaze drift over toward Josh Redigger. Like everyone else, Mr. Earle had been giving Josh his space for the last few weeks, in light of things. Ryan could tell his teacher was wondering if it was time to bring Josh back into the fold. But the kid wasn't ready. It wasn't time.

"Fear," Ryan said.

Mr. Earle looked over at Ryan, straightening his glasses. "Continue."

"They used the stories to scare kids."

"Why?"

Ryan shrugged. It was obvious. "To make them behave. Hansel and Gretel: Don't take candy from strangers. The Boy Who Cried Wolf: Don't lie to grown-ups. Parents always think that kids aren't ready to be scared of the real things, so they make up monsters for us to practice on."

"Understandable, don't you think?" Mr. Earle said.

"Understandable," Ryan said. "But wrong."

Mr. Earle gave Ryan a little "go on" nod of the head.

"They think they're protecting us," Ryan continued. "But they're really just protecting themselves. Whether we're scared of a wicked witch or the creepy guy in the van, we're no better off. *We're* still scared. It just makes *them* feel better to have us scared of something that isn't real."

Mr. Earle looked at Ryan for a moment. "Okay," he said. "Good stuff. Now, can anyone think of any legends or folklore that we have right here in Cliffs Donnelly?"

"Crybaby Bridge?" Paige offered.

"That's over in Abbeyville," said Jamie.

"So? It's still kind of local."

"Sasquatch."

"Give it up, man. Besides, Bigfoot's Canadian."

"Sasquatch! And his migratory patterns clearly stretch into Michigan—"

"He doesn't have any migratory patterns, Aaron, because he doesn't exist!"

"Shut up, Jamie!"

"Thompkins Well," Ernest Wilmette offered.

"Yes," Mr. Earle said enthusiastically. "Do you know the story, Ernest?"

"Only that my grandpa told me a long time ago people used to throw coins in it and make wishes."

"That's right. The legend dates back to the late 1800s. A local merchant by the name of Ezekiel Thompkins went to the well and threw in a coin. His infant grandson was very sick and wasn't expected to live through the night. The old man wished for death to take him instead and spare the child. He then went home and died that night in his sleep. The baby recovered and the legend of Thompkins Well was born."

"Do you believe any of that?" Jamie said.

"Well, Ezekiel Thompkins was a real person; his name is all over the city archives. And he did die shortly after his grandson was born."

"Yes," said Ernest Wilmette. "But do you believe the story?"

Mr. Earle thought for a moment. "I don't know, Ernest. I believe in hope. And I believe in love . . ." Mr. Earle closed his eyes and spread out his arms and started to sing:

"And I believe that children are the future
Teach them well and let them lead the way . . ."

The class groaned and the bell rang. Everyone got up from their seats as Mr. Earle dismissed them, still in song:

"Enjoy your lunch and eat your vegetables
Then on to math and learn some decimals . . ."

TOMMY BRICKS

Sixth grade didn't have recess anymore, but after lunch Ernest and his classmates were allowed outside for a while before resuming afternoon classes. Some kids, like Ryan Hardy, would play football on the field, but Ernest rarely joined in. Usually, he would just sit under a tree and read. Sometimes, Lizzy MacComber would pass by and ask him what he was reading, just to be polite. Ernest usually responded by mumbling the title as he looked down at the ground or, worse, by giving Lizzy a lengthy, rambling description of the book in question.

Across the yard Winston Patil sat by himself at one of the picnic tables, sketching in a drawing tablet. Ernest had always been curious about what Winston was drawing, and once or twice he thought about going over and asking. But he never did.

Winston's head was buried in his drawing tablet, so he didn't notice Tommy Bricks walking over until Tommy reached down and snatched the tablet. Winston grabbed for it, but Tommy was too fast. Tommy started looking through the pages and talking loudly.

"What kind of lame drawing is this?" Tommy laughed.

Kids were starting to crowd around them. It was becoming a thing.

Winston reached for the tablet, the token effort of resistance required by the bullied. "Please," he said. "Just give it back."

"Why? So you can draw more lousy pictures? I'd be doing you a favor if I just tore these all up."

Winston panicked then and lunged for the tablet. Tommy easily shoved him back and gave him a hard look that told him he better not try that again.

"Stop!" a voice said sternly. The voice was loud, commanding, and it belonged to Ernest. Everyone turned, stunned that he was the one who had spoken up. Ernest was pretty stunned, himself. Even more surprising, he was actually walking toward Tommy Bricks, a fellow sixth grader but still the toughest, meanest, and scariest kid in Rod Serling Middle School.

Tommy stared at Ernest, his mouth half-open as if wondering

where all his curse words (along with the natural order of things) had just gone. If he were a computer, the center of his face would have a rainbow-colored wheel spinning over it. "What . . ." he finally managed.

"Just give it back, Tommy. C'mon."

"C'mon? C'mon?" Tommy repeated the words with growing emphasis, as if they guided him back to how moments like this were supposed to go. "Listen, rich boy. My daddy doesn't work for your daddy. And that means I don't have to take any crap from you." He stepped closer to Ernest, in his face. Well, he would have been if they had matched up face-to-face; it was really more like face-to-bottom-of-the-sternum.

Tommy stood there for a moment and pretended to think. "Huh. I guess it also means there's no reason not to beat you into the ground right now."

GAME, INTERRUPTED

Ryan loved playing football. Because when Ryan played football, he forgot about everything else. School, chores, a baby brother who hated him, and Mrs. Haemmerle's piece-of-junk lawn mower.

The way his mom and dad had been avoiding each other

around the house. The way they both got quiet around each other when they couldn't. That was harder to shake.

Last night, he'd heard them through the walls, arguing in their room.

"I don't want to hear it, Doug. I just want to go to sleep."

His dad said, "Sure, go ahead. You sleep."

"No one asked you to spend all evening in the den drinking beer and watching that trash."

"I had two beers," his dad said. "Can't a guy have two beers after—"

"It's not the beers," his mom said. "And you know it. It's those pasty talking heads you love so much, and the vile, hateful things they—"

"You know, if that idiot Bilkes doesn't come through, Wilmette's gonna sell the factory," his dad said, cutting her off. "He won't have a choice."

"I know," his mom said quietly.

Ryan really wished he could forget about that conversation. And on a good day, when the game was really moving, when the teams were evenly matched and every play really counted, he could. For a while.

Today was one of those days. Ryan threw for one touchdown and ran for another. He made an interception and four tackles.

And then the game stopped.

Over by the picnic tables a crowd had started forming in that way that can only mean a fight is breaking out. And no football game, no matter how much fun, can compete with a fight.

He saw Tommy Bricks first, because he was practically a head taller than the crowd of kids surrounding him. No surprise there; he was always getting in fights.

Ryan wondered who the poor chump was this time.

ERNEST STANDS HIS GROUND

Ernest remained rooted to his spot as Tommy stared him down. He didn't have much choice: His legs were shaking so hard that he didn't think he could move them.

Adults always say to stand up to bullies. The implication being that if you stand up to a bully, the bully will back down. Ernest thought about this morning's Council and realized now that this, too, was a fairy tale of a kind. You don't stand up to a bully to make him back down.

You stand up to him because maybe, if you're lucky, he'll decide that beating you up is too much hassle and move on to someone else. You stand up to him because it's worse not to. Which is a different truth entirely.

Adults also say that deep down all bullies are really scared themselves and that's why they act like bullies. That may be true, Ernest thought. But it's just plain useless information.

Because whatever Tommy Bricks might really be afraid of, it sure wasn't Ernest Wilmette.

RYAN (RELUCTANTLY) DOES THE RIGHT THING

This is bad.

That was all Ryan could think when he saw Ernest Wilmette squaring off with Tommy Bricks in front of the entire sixth grade.

This is really bad.

Because Ernest Wilmette was small and uncoordinated and injury-prone. He had once ridden his bike into a parked car. In his own garage.

Because Ernest was the boss's son. And he was about to get pulverized. Out of the corner of his eye, Ryan saw Lizzy heading inside to get a teacher. But even if she ran, he knew she wouldn't make it back in time to stop the worst of it.

This is really, really—

"Leave him alone, Tommy."

I'm an idiot, Ryan thought to himself. A suicidal idiot. On my tombstone it will say, "Here lies Ryan Hardy. Son, brother, dummy with a death wish."

But he had no choice. Tommy Bricks could seriously hurt Ernest. And Ryan's dad would want to know why he hadn't stopped it.

So here he was, stopping it.

"Stay out of this, Hardy."

Ryan positioned himself between Tommy and Ernest. Ryan wasn't nearly as big as Tommy. But they came from the same neighborhood—they weren't sheltered North Side kids. Maybe Tommy would just leave it.

"Fine, then," Tommy Bricks said. "Let's throw down."

Maybe not.

Then Ms. Hackwell, their science teacher, came outside to see what all the trouble was about. Ernest looked like he'd never been so glad to see another person in his entire life.

But Ryan knew the feeling would be short-lived. After all, Tommy Bricks wasn't the kind of kid who let things go. Ms. Hackwell would only be a temporary reprieve from the predicament that Ernest had brought upon himself and, now, Ryan. Though Tommy backed down for the teacher, he still got in the last word. Well, two words, actually.

After. School.

4

LIZZY'S DILEMMA

Lizzy spent the afternoon trying to decide what she should do. Or, rather, what she would do. She knew what she *should* do. She should tell Mr. Earle what had happened at lunch.

And if only Ernest and Winston had been involved, that was exactly what she would have done. But Ryan was a different story. Lizzy and Ryan and Tommy all lived in the same neighborhood, and where they were from, you didn't go crying to adults to fix your problems. And you didn't tattle, ever.

It was the code of the South Side, and if Ryan found out she went to the teachers on his behalf he'd be furious. He truly might never speak to her again.

Not that he was speaking to her all that much now.

Lizzy knew what her mom would say. Her mom would want her to tell, to do what was best for Ryan even if it meant he stopped talking to her forever. To do the right thing.

Her mom always did the right thing. But her mom was alone. Her mom cried in her bedroom. If that's what doing the right thing got you, Lizzy couldn't help but wonder, then what was the point?

RYAN HARDY REFLECTS ON HIS IMPENDING DOOM

For the first hour or so after lunch, Ryan's mind worked overtime trying to figure out what to do. Math and science were one big blur.

Maybe, he thought, he could try to reason with Tommy. He could tell Tommy that he was just trying to keep him out of trouble, that beating up a North Side kid—especially Ernest Wilmette, the poster boy for North Side kids—would get him suspended, even expelled. It would be a fair point, actually.

But Tommy wouldn't care. Tommy was the youngest of three boys and they were all mean. Scary mean. Crazy mean. Tommy had one brother in jail and another brother in the Marines, and that's only because the judge told the other brother it was either that or jail for him, too. Even the parents were mean. The dad drank a lot and nearly went to jail himself for cracking a guy's head open in the Taco Bell parking lot. The mom, Ryan heard, kept a knife in her boot. People avoided them.

Ryan had, too. Until today.

ERNEST IS RESOLVED

It had occurred to Ernest that he could probably slip away from this mess entirely. And as much as it shamed him to admit it, a big part of him really wanted to do just that.

But he couldn't. He knew Ryan had only stepped in because Mr. Hardy worked for Ernest's dad and Ryan felt he had no choice but to stick up for Ernest. He couldn't let Ryan literally fight his battles for him.

After the last bell, Ernest stepped outside the school determined to fight Tommy Bricks. Terrified beyond measure, of course, but determined. At least he'd be able to look himself in the mirror in the morning.

Provided Tommy didn't give him a blinding concussion.

RYAN CALLS AN AUDIBLE

When the last bell rang, Ryan went to his locker, gathered his things, and, without looking at anyone, walked purposefully down the hall and out of the school.

Down the big hill about two blocks from the school campus, a vacant lot sat next to a small corner market. Ryan figured that's where Tommy would be waiting for him.

He barely got twenty yards past the school entrance when Ernest intercepted him.

Ryan said, "What do you want?"

"You don't have to fight Tommy," Ernest replied with trembling conviction. "I started this."

"Yeah, you did."

"And I'm sorry you got involved. But I'm going to make it right."

"Really," Ryan said, almost amused. "How are you going to do that?"

"I'm . . . I'm going to fight Tommy Bricks."

Ryan laughed out loud. "No. You're not. Go home, Ernest," he said. "It's best for everyone if you do."

Ernest frowned. Ryan could tell he'd hurt the kid's feelings, but he didn't really care. "I won't."

Ernest wasn't budging. Stupid little rich kid. Stupid, stubborn, clueless little rich kid.

Ryan had to come up with a new plan, fast. He considered his options. But the only way he could think to stop Ernest from trying to fight Tommy Bricks would be to beat Ernest up himself. Which, at the moment, was kind of tempting . . .

"Fine," Ryan said as he grabbed Ernest by the arm and led him back toward the school.

LIZZY'S OWN AFTER-SCHOOL PROBLEMS

Lizzy tried to find Ryan after school. Not that she knew what she would do if she found him. She finally spotted him walking down the hill toward the vacant lot, then saw him arguing with Ernest.

Should she go over to them, find a teacher, maybe—

HONK! HONK, HONK, HONK!

"Lizzy! C'mon!! Geez!" The honking was from Aunt Patty's super-sized SUV. The impatient caterwauling was from Lizzy's cousin Chelsea.

Right. Lizzy's mom had texted her at lunch that she had to cover an extra shift at the hospital. Which meant an afternoon with . . . them.

Lizzy took one last look down the hill but couldn't see Ryan or Ernest anymore.

"Lizzy! For reals!! Move your butt!"

She looked back at the SUV and wondered if she wouldn't rather be fighting Tommy Bricks instead.

WINSTON PATIL WALKS HOME

Last week, Winston Patil had an argument with his mother. Well, not an argument, exactly. He'd never argue with his mother, or anyone, for that matter. What Winston really did was persistently ask for something, in a reasoned, measured tone of voice, until his mother finally gave in.

Winston had wanted to walk home from school on his own, and this worried Mrs. Patil. A lot. That it worried his mom frustrated Winston. A lot. When they lived in Chicago she hadn't worried this much, and that was a big city. But ever since they'd moved to Cliffs Donnelly, Winston's mother seemed nervous all the time.

It was Winston's father who'd eventually convinced his mother to let him walk home from school. Dr. Patil was an esteemed and successful surgeon who traveled all over the world, who reveled in seeing new places and meeting new people, so perhaps he felt it would be hypocritical not to back his son's attempts to travel the mere three-quarters of a mile from Rod Serling Middle School to their house.

Curiously, it had been the globe-trotting Dr. Patil's idea to leave Chicago and move the family to Cliffs Donnelly, Ohio. Mrs. Patil told her husband he was the smartest fool who ever was. They could have lived anywhere. She begged him not to leave Chicago, or if he wanted to move, to at least choose another major city. But Dr. Patil had always wanted to live in a small town, preferably one surrounded by lots of fields and open spaces. Winston's father loved America. The people, the land, the very *idea* of it. Loved it so much he broke with hundreds of years of family tradition and named his eldest son just about the least Indian name imaginable.

And now here they were. Cliffs Donnelly, Ohio. Winston's father called it the heartland. His mother called it the middle of nowhere.

Though grateful to his father for taking his side about walking home from school, Winston agreed with his mother about Cliffs Donnelly. He'd never say so to his father, but this move was a mistake. They didn't fit in here; they didn't belong. When they'd first arrived, Winston knew it would be hard to be the new kid, especially in a small town like this where the other kids had all been going to school together for years. But after a few weeks he realized it was something more than that.

Because deep down, he knew why his mom was nervous. They were *different* here. Really different. They stood out. In Chicago, Mrs. Patil could wear a sari to the grocery store and it wasn't a big deal. Chicago had all kinds: Lots of people looked differently, dressed differently, and talked differently.

Here there was just the one kind, and it sure wasn't him. The other kids all avoided him at school. They weren't mean about it, generally—they just gave him space. Lots of space.

He had his drawing, at least. It was his favorite thing to do, and he was good at it. He used to spend hours sitting on the benches at the Art Institute, copying paintings in his sketchbook. But there wasn't much to sketch here, unless you really had a thing for flat landscapes and stalks of wheat. Still, it did make being alone easier. He could bury his head in his drawings as he sat by himself during lunch. He was lonely, but at least he was occupied.

As Winston exited the school, he realized he wasn't sure where he stood on the concept of irony, much less the whole idea of experiencing new places and people. But the run-in with Tommy Bricks during lunch, coming on the first day he was to walk home on his own, did seem to suggest the universe had a cruel sense of humor.

SNEAKING AWAY

"Wait," Ernest said. "Where are we going?"

He and Ryan had just cut through the teachers' parking lot and were making their way down the steeply declining hill behind the school. Ryan still held Ernest by the arm and looked over his shoulder every twenty feet or so.

"We're going to cut through the Nature Preserve. I know the trails. It'll spit us out at North Side Park." The Nature Preserve was littered with trails—some new, some very old, but all seldom used except by science teachers taking their kids out for a free field trip or teenagers who wanted to smoke cigarettes and complain about how misunderstood they were.

"But . . . you mean we're running away?"

"No, we're sneaking away," Ryan said, looking back toward the school one more time. "Running away is what we'll be doing if Tommy spots us before we hit the tree line."

Ernest had a follow-up question or two about this course of action, but the fact that Ryan was already disappearing inside the preserve sent a pretty clear signal that the matter was not open to debate.

5

READING FACES

On the way home, Winston couldn't help noticing Tommy Bricks at the vacant lot next to the drugstore, pacing back and forth with clenched fists. Winston meant to look away before Tommy could see him, but it was too late. They locked eyes, and for an instant Winston thought, with a strange matter-of-factness, that he was a dead man.

Tommy's eyes narrowed, but then his face did something weird—it kind of winced. And then Tommy, *he* looked away. Winston couldn't believe it. He doubted Tommy Bricks had ever looked away first in his life.

One survival skill you pick up rather quickly when you're different (and especially when you're not just different, but *conspicuously* different, like the only twelve-year-old Indian American for a fifty-mile radius) is a heightened ability to read people. When Tommy first took the drawing tablet at lunch, Winston had thought he saw something in the bully's eyes that told Winston he didn't really mean what he was saying about the drawings. The anger was real, Winston didn't doubt that, but he was pretty sure that anger wasn't actually about him.

Winston also wondered if Tommy was pretty good at reading people, too. Because the minute these thoughts crystallized in Winston's mind, Tommy had shoved him and threatened to do worse.

And so Winston wasn't about to make the same mistake twice. As soon as Tommy looked way, Winston made sure to be long gone from the vacant lot before the big kid looked back.

INTO THE WOODS

Ernest followed Ryan into the Nature Preserve. It was a bright day, but barely twenty feet into the trees the sunlight gave way to the dimness of shade.

"You know," Ernest said, trying to sound nonchalant and not doing a bang-up job of it. "They say there are devil worshippers in these woods."

"There aren't any devil worshippers in the woods, Ernest."

"How do you know?"

Ryan shook his head in disbelief. "That's just a rumor burn-outs from the high school started so they won't be bothered when they come here to smoke cigarettes and drink peppermint schnapps."

"Oh," Ernest said. "Why peppermint schnapps?"

"I don't know, Ernest!" Ryan snapped.

They walked for a while without talking after that.

"What happens now?" Ernest asked.

"I told you," Ryan said. "There's a trail that will spit us out by North Side Park. You can walk home from there."

"Yeah. But what about you?"

"What about me?"

"Well," Ernest started. "You live on the other side of town. That's at least a couple of miles from there."

"Sounds about right."

"You could come with me, and my mom could give you a ride home."

"I'll be fine," Ryan said.

THE CAVE

Ryan wished Ernest wouldn't talk so much. Truth be told, he didn't know these trails that well and needed to concentrate.

Plus, he had bigger things on his mind. Because even after he got Ernest safely home, he would still have Tommy Bricks to deal with.

Ryan figured he'd walk back past the vacant lot to see if Tommy was still there. If not, Ryan guessed Tommy would be waiting to jump him somewhere along the way back to the South Side.

"Wait." Ernest stopped on the trail, the metaphor of a light bulb illuminating over his head. "You're still going to fight him, aren't you?"

Ryan turned around, irritated. What was it with this kid? "I don't know, Ernest."

"But that's why you won't take a ride home, isn't it?"

"Don't worry about it."

"You are. Okay, I'm going back."

Ryan looked around, confused suddenly. "No, stop."

"Ryan, I mean it. I'm not letting you—"

"Just shut up a minute," Ryan said. "I think I'm lost."

Up ahead the trail curved and seemed to disappear into the deeper woods.

Ernest moved ahead of Ryan and started following the curve.

"Hey, where are you going?"

"The preserve's not that big," Ernest said. "We can't get *that* lost." He was running farther around the bend now. "Whoa, cool," Ryan heard from up ahead.

When Ryan caught Ernest, who was now halfway up a hill about twenty yards off the trail, he was standing before a small cave, no more than three feet high. All around the opening, there was thick brush; it would be easy to miss.

"Let's go inside," Ernest said.

Ryan tried to stop him, but Ernest was already climbing into the opening. Every minute with this kid is like babysitting, Ryan thought.

Ryan went into the cave after him. For a few yards the tunnel was a tight fit, but then it opened up to walking height. Way ahead, a hundred feet or so, the faint glow of daylight lit a larger cavern.

"Ryan, c'mon. You've got to see this."

Ryan found Ernest at the end of the cavern, in a pit about the size of a small room. The walls were covered in thick moss and the ground was wet . . . and shiny.

Ernest bent down and picked up something small and metallic. "It's a coin," he said, running his fingers across the ground. "They're all coins."

Ryan looked up. The pit narrowed into a shaft that became

perfectly cylindrical at the top. Broken, rotted boards covered most of the circular opening, but thin streaks of sunlight snuck through the gaps.

"We're in a well," Ryan said. He heard the faint sounds of kids playing, and then it all came together. "We must be near North Side Park. This is Thompkins Well."

AMBER

Chelsea had a little sister, Amber, who was a year younger than Lizzy. The sisters were a study in opposites. Chelsea was excessive—everything about her demanded attention. She was, simply put, just too much. Like her clothes, which were loud and desperately trendy. And her makeup, which was heavy and smothering. And her hair, which was too glazed and strangely vertical (but on this point Lizzy had to concede that her cousin's hair would probably be gorgeous if only it were liberated from the merciless deluge of hair care products shellacked upon it).

Amber, conversely, had perfected the art of making people forget she was even in the room. She had slick straight hair that clung to her scalp and slid tightly down her back in a way that reminded Lizzy of an otter shooting up a river. While Chelsea had never grasped the concept of an "indoor voice," Amber could speak and still, somehow, seem to avoid making any discernible noise. She even dressed quietly, in largely natural, muted colors, all the easier for blending in with walls or disappearing into crowds. In another life, she had no doubt been an excellent ninja.

Once they were back at Aunt Patty's, Chelsea decided to give Lizzy a makeover. Lizzy tried to object, but Chelsea had already dashed up the stairs to the master bathroom and come back with a shopping bag stuffed with cosmetics.

"Mom won't let us use her personal stash," Chelsea said while combing through a bottomless supply of little tubes, jars, and bottles. "But she gets *a lot* of samples."

Lizzy was cornered; Chelsea would throw a fit if she didn't go along. Adults like to tell kids to just walk away when faced with an unpleasant person or situation. Useless advice, Lizzy thought, if you don't have somewhere to walk away to.

THOMPKINS WELL

Winston was not a superstitious person. Legends, folklore, the mysterious and unexplained, none of that ever really caught his attention that much. So Mr. Earle's story in Council today about Thompkins Well hadn't registered as anything more than that. A story.

But it had been an odd day. Ernest, the one boy in class smaller and frailer than Winston himself, had actually tried to stick up for him. And then Ryan, a kid who was only slightly less surly and disagreeable than Tommy, had come out of nowhere to stick up for Ernest. Not to mention the way Tommy had looked away from Winston at the vacant lot . . .

Something strange was in the air.

Such was Winston's state of mind as he passed North Side Park on his way home and spotted, at the far edge of the park, just in front of the tree line for the Nature Preserve, Thompkins Well. He reconsidered the story Mr. Earle had told in class, about the old man and his wish.

And, for once, followed his imagination a little bit.

Over the decades, the well had fallen into serious disrepair. The stonework was solid but grimy with moss, particularly along the bottom. There was a wooden canopy over the top that was half-rotted from the rain. Across the mouth were some wood planks, presumably to keep kids from falling down the well. But the slats had grown brittle and thin, and two of them, the ones in the middle, were missing altogether.

Deep down, Winston still knew that what he was about to do was foolish. But he pulled a quarter out of his pocket anyway.

6

INSIDE THE WELL

"Thompkins Well?" Ernest said. "We're *inside* Thompkins Well?"

"Yeah, I think so." Ryan picked up one of the coins. "Explains all the change. Some of these are pretty old."

"Hello?" A voice echoed around them; it seemed to come from the well itself.

Ryan and Ernest froze.

"Ryan . . ." Ernest whispered, his voice quivering urgently. "The well is haunted."

"No, it's not," Ryan said with less certainty than he'd hoped to muster.

"Um, this is Winston," the voice echoed again.

Ernest whimpered. "Ryan, the ghost is named Winston."

"Ernest, shut up," Ryan snapped.

The mystery voice kept talking. Apparently it couldn't hear them.

"This is silly. I know. But I heard your story in school today, about how you granted a wish to an old man named Thompkins and saved his baby grandson from dying."

It was starting to make sense to Ryan now. "That's Winston Patil," he whispered.

"From school?" Ernest looked confused.

"Oh, sorry," Winston said from above. "Almost forgot." A quarter dropped down from above, smacking Ernest on the head. Ernest looked up the shaft, catching on.

"So, as you probably guessed, I'd like to make a wish, too. It's not as big as the Ezekiel Thompkins wish. It's not life-or-death or anything. I'm new here and, well, it's kind of hard to fit in. I'm not asking to be popular or anything, but maybe . . . someone my own age to talk to would be nice. I just . . . I'd like a friend."

Ryan felt awkward hearing Winston's wish. He knew it was an accident, but still, this was something private, and Ryan felt dirty for eavesdropping on it.

"Anyway, thanks for listening," Winston said after a long silence.

"Wow," Ernest said after Winston had walked away.

Ryan said, "Let's get out of here."

"I never realized Winston felt that way," said Ernest as they inched back through the tunnel.

"Seriously?" Ryan scoffed. "Kid buries his head in his sketchbook every day at lunch. Never talks to anyone, barely looks up."

Ryan started leading them up the trail.

"I know," said Ernest. "But at least now we can do something about it."

"Do? What are we going to do?"

"Well, we can . . . you know. Befriend him."

"*Befriend* him?"

"Yeah, become his friend."

Ryan shook his head. "It doesn't work like that."

"It could."

"Yeah? How? We just go up to him and say, 'Hi, Winston, let's be friends'?"

Ernest started to answer, but Ryan plowed ahead. "And what's this 'we' you keep talking about? I mean, *we* aren't even friends."

"I know . . ."

"You don't," Ryan started, then stopped. How did you even go about explaining the world to someone like Ernest? "What happens if you discover you don't like him? Or he doesn't like you?"

"Doesn't mean we—I—shouldn't try."

"Like you tried this afternoon with Tommy?"

Ryan marched ahead up the trail, with Ernest following quietly behind. The path snaked along, switchbacking several times, and Ryan was sure they would wind up completely lost and stuck in the woods for the night.

This is what you get for trying to help people, he thought.

Ryan had always pegged Ernest as a sheltered, naive, rich kid. But now he realized it was way worse than that. Ernest Wilmette wasn't just rich, sheltered, and naive. Ernest was a dreamer.

And dreamers, Ryan was discovering, are really exhausting people.

MAKEOVER NIGHTMARE

Chelsea started with foundation, a lot of foundation, applying it with such a heavy hand that before long, Lizzy looked like one of the Oompa Loompas from *Willy Wonka and the Chocolate Factory*. Chelsea followed this with enough blush and blue eye shadow that Lizzy could have been mistaken for a police cruiser if she left the house. And the glare of her unnaturally iridescent hot-pink lip gloss could have guided a wayward plane in for an emergency landing.

Amber, as usual, said nothing. She just watched with a faint smile that Lizzy suspected tried to hide equal doses of disgust and sympathy.

Chelsea stepped back to gauge her work. She nodded appraisingly.

"Not bad. You know, Lizzy," she said, "you could be half-way decent-looking if you tried." Chelsea contemplated some more. "Have to do something about those clothes, though."

Fortunately for Lizzy, Chelsea's fashion intervention would have to wait. Aunt Patty interrupted to tell them that Lizzy's mom was here to pick her up. It was slow at the hospital and her mom had knocked off early.

Upon seeing Lizzy, her mom betrayed a quick look of shock, but didn't say anything about it on the ride home.

Lizzy wasn't sure what to make of her mom's silence, except that it made her angry. *How could you not say something about this?* she wanted to yell. *I look like an idiot! I look like the Joker's inner child!*

But her mom just drove them home, humming to herself like she was in her own little world.

Maybe she was too tired to care, Lizzy thought. Or worse, maybe she thought it wasn't that bad.

OUT OF THE WOODS

Sooner than expected, the trail opened up on the far side of the park. Ryan hid it pretty well, but he was relieved to have found their way back out. "You can get yourself home from here?"

Ernest nodded. "Sure you don't want that ride?"

"I'm sure," Ryan said. "Thanks, though."

Before Ernest could respond, Ryan turned and started walking the opposite way. A few minutes later, he doubled back to the vacant lot. It was kind of out of the way now, but he figured he had to check.

As expected, Tommy wasn't there anymore. Odds were that he'd be waiting for Ryan somewhere along their walk home. It was a good two miles from North Side Park to Ryan's block. By the time he'd made it to Mrs. Haemmerle's house, though, there was still no sign of Tommy, and Ryan started to nurture a seedling of hope that maybe . . .

"Where you going, Hardy?"

Ryan had to stop doing that to himself.

"I wasn't ducking you, Tommy. I had to . . ." Ryan began, then stopped. Tommy didn't care. "I wasn't ducking you."

Tommy squinted at him. "I believe you," he said.

Ryan looked around. They were standing on the sidewalk

directly in front of Mrs. Haemmerle's bay window. If she saw them fighting, she might freak and literally have a heart attack. He was about to ask Tommy if they could move it down a few houses when Tommy said, "Why'd you get in my face like that? Because your dad works for Wilmette's dad?"

Ryan shrugged. "I don't know. Maybe. You ever do something and not know why?"

Tommy looked surprised, both by the nature of the question and that a question was actually asked of him. Ryan supposed Tommy didn't get many questions. The only conversations he had probably consisted of adults yelling at him or kids begging for mercy.

"I guess so," Tommy said. "Don't let it happen again." He turned around and walked away without saying another word.

Ryan made his way to the curb and leaned up against one of Mrs. Haemmerle's empty garbage bins as he waited patiently for his knees to stop buckling.

LIZZY AT THE WINDOW

Lizzy had been sitting by her front window for over half an hour. She'd been there since the fifth minute she and her mom got home, hoping to catch sight of Ryan. (She spent the first four scrubbing off the pounds of makeup her cousin had spackled onto her face.) Before she'd climbed into Aunt Patty's SUV, Lizzy had caught a glimpse of Ryan leading Ernest into the woods behind their school. Lizzy had been relieved at the time, but she was too smart to kid herself that Ryan was out of the woods, so to speak. She had already spotted Tommy loitering across the street from Mrs. Haemmerle's house.

Lizzy finally saw Ryan come around the corner. When he got to Mrs. Haemmerle's, Tommy crossed the street, blocking Ryan's path on the sidewalk.

Though Lizzy wouldn't tell at school, at home was a different matter. At home she had options. Her mom was in the other room, on the phone, and if anything happened, Lizzy could go and get her. Tommy wouldn't cross Lizzy's mom—she had set his arm for him when he broke it falling off a utility pole three summers ago.

Though Lizzy could see the boys talking, she was too far away to make out what they were saying. It was a brief conversation, noteworthy because at the end of it Tommy walked away, leaving Ryan visibly shaken but otherwise upright.

Lizzy could hardly believe her eyes at this borderline miraculous turn of events. Consumed with a giddiness that practically made her squeal with delight, she went to find her mom.

"Mom," she called, running into her mom's bedroom. "Hey, Mom!"

Her mom, still on the phone, was startled. "Lizzy, are you okay?"

Lizzy realized she was interrupting. "Oh, sorry. It can wait."

"I'll be out in a couple of minutes," her mom said, blushing a little as she covered the bottom of the phone with her hand. Lizzy nodded. Her mom closed the door gently as Lizzy returned to the living room. Most days, Lizzy's keen eye for detail would have picked up on her mom's curious behavior, but she was so relieved at Ryan's lack of pummeling that she failed to notice.

ERNEST TRIES AGAIN

Ernest's dad was still at the factory when Ernest got home. He and his mom had leftovers. The house felt empty as they ate, their silverware loudly clinking against their plates.

After dinner Ernest went up to his room. He wondered if Ryan was right about trying to make friends with Winston. Ryan saved his butt today. Twice. Because Ernest had stuck his nose where it didn't belong. Maybe there was a lesson there.

Probably there was a lesson there.

Either way, Ernest couldn't simply forget about what Winston had said at the well. Maybe you couldn't become somebody's friend just because they needed one. But what if you could? If there was a chance . . .

Ernest's gaze drifted across the room. Leaning up against his desk, under an umbrella of light from his desk lamp, was the art set he'd taken from Grandpa Eddie's attic yesterday. Ernest had spent much of the day in fear for his life, a distraction that had made him forget all about the art set.

But now, like before in the attic, it seemed to beckon him. Only this time Ernest knew what to do. He picked up the art set and put it in his backpack.

Maybe he could show it to Winston at lunch to break the ice. Ernest was awful at art. He could ask Winston for pointers or something.

It wasn't a terrible idea.

7

A BRIEF STUDY OF LOCKERS

Every student at Rod Serling Middle School was afraid of Tommy Bricks.

Tommy knew as much. How could he not? For a time, during the first couple weeks of school, Tommy had even tested the waters by walking down the halls and giving hard looks to all the biggest kids, challenging them, calling them out with his eyes. He figured someone would do something.

But they all looked away.

Tommy knew why. They expected him to be like Wade or his dad. The truth of it, though, was that Tommy didn't enjoy making people afraid of him. It wasn't fun, and it didn't make him feel good. But it felt better than having people look down on him. Or feel sorry for him. Nothing was worse than that. Tommy wasn't like Wade or his dad: He wasn't mean. That said, he'd rather have everyone hate him—he'd rather hurt them all—than have one person ever feel sorry for him.

Yesterday had been different.

Because yesterday he really had been mean, and he didn't know why. Tommy had nothing against Winston and actually thought his drawings were really good. Taking Winston's tablet, saying those things—it'd just started happening, and Tommy hadn't known how to make it stop.

Then that Wilmette kid had stepped in. Something about that kid, the way he looked at Tommy, got him really mad. Mad in a way that scared him. At first he'd thought Wilmette was looking down on him, but it wasn't that. It was more complicated, like he had looked *inside* Tommy, had seen who he really was.

It had set something off in Tommy, something he didn't think he could control. If Ryan Hardy hadn't stepped in . . .

And that's when it hit him, hard like a kick to the chest. He knew now why Sam had to leave. Tommy understood. When everyone expects the worst from you, sooner or later you're going to give it to them.

And yesterday, Tommy very nearly had.

Which, of course, made what he was doing today all the more stupid. What he had in his backpack this morning could get him suspended, even expelled.

If anyone caught him they'd probably call the police, say he was bringing weapons to school. And technically, they wouldn't be wrong. The things he had in his backpack could be, strictly speaking, considered weapons.

They weren't weapons, though. They were tools.

Sam's tools.

One day, a little over a month ago and just a couple of days into the new school year, Tommy noticed something while throwing his books in his locker.

As the books crashed into the back wall, they made a sound that was just a little bit different, a little bit off. The sound he heard was too metallic, had too much tinny echo behind it. Tommy stuck his head into the locker and tapped lightly in several different spots. As he suspected, they made roughly the same sound, and he knew why.

Over the next week, Tommy listened as the other kids nearby worked their lockers, and he heard pretty much the same thing. None of the other kids heard it, but that wasn't surprising. Tommy's ear was trained to hear when things didn't sound right. At home, he was the one who fixed the squeaky hinge, the leaky faucet. He was the one who stopped the washer from making that high, whirring sound during the rinse cycle.

Well, he and his brother Sam.

Sam taught him how to fix things, how to use tools. His brother had an awesome set of tools and could fix anything. Tommy picked the lessons up fast. But while Sam was obsessed with how things worked, how pieces fit together and operated, Tommy's imagination kept looking for different things to do with all the parts and pieces, ways to put them together to build something new.

Tommy had a hunch about the lockers. At least halfway down the hall, he figured, there was nothing solid behind them, no concrete, no drywall even, just open space.

And it gave him an idea.

Tommy had refused to say goodbye to Sam on the day his brother left for the Marines. Sam had been with Wade the night Wade had gotten so drunk that he'd started beating up a bartender who wouldn't give him any more to drink.

Sam had tried to stop his brother, but in the end it had taken two policemen and their billy clubs to bring Wade down.

Wade had been charged with two felony counts of assault. Sam had signed up for the Marines the same day Wade was sent to prison, which only added to the misconception that he'd been sent away, too. That the Bricks boys were all no good.

Tommy hadn't understood why Sam had to leave. It wasn't fair. He'd run away, leaving Tommy behind.

Tommy wouldn't look at him when they dropped Sam off at the bus station, not even when his dad threatened to give him a smack if he didn't drop it already. When Sam hugged him good-bye, Tommy didn't hug him back.

"My tools," Sam whispered in his little brother's ear. "I put them in your closet. Take care of them for me?"

Tommy didn't turn to look at Sam, but he couldn't help nodding at this request.

That was near the end of summer vacation, and Tommy hadn't thought much about the tools since. Then, a few weeks ago, he came across his dad rummaging through the garage. It was late afternoon, around the time when his dad usually left for the bars.

"You seen your brother's tools?" he barked at Tommy.

Tommy shook his head. His father scowled and went back to searching the garage. When he came up empty, he stormed away and stayed out all night.

Tommy's father had never fixed anything in his life. If he wanted Sam's tools, it sure wasn't to use them. It was to sell them, for beer money.

That was why Sam had hidden them in Tommy's closet, why he'd asked Tommy to take care of them. Sam knew that sooner or later their dad would be looking to hock his tools.

And while Tommy's father was not a particularly smart man, he was a crafty one. If Tommy wanted to protect those tools, he had to get them out of the house.

Last week Tommy had brought Sam's punch kit and nibbler

shears to school and tested his hunch about the locker. At the end of the day, he waited in the bathroom for all the kids and teachers to leave, and for that old janitor to finally pass by with his push broom. Then he went to his locker and carefully carved out a clean, two-foot rectangle from the locker's back panel. With a penlight in hand, he poked his head into the hole and looked around.

Just as he had suspected, there was a long pocket of dead space, wide enough to stand in, spanning the length of the hallway.

He taped the rectangular plate back over the hole. Then the next day he installed a top hinge, creasing the edges of the back plate and the locker's side panels so that it swung open neatly and smoothly, like a little doggie door.

Tommy had originally planned to bring one or two of the tools to school each day, but if his father found some of them in the meantime, then he'd know Tommy had hidden the rest, which would be very bad for Tommy. No, Tommy would have to start moving the tools in bulk, a backpack full at a time. Starting today.

It was risky, especially after yesterday, when he nearly took that Wilmette kid apart. If Wilmette had gone crying to his rich daddy after school, then it was a sure bet that today Tommy would be yanked into the principal's office the second he set foot on school property.

Nevertheless, he decided to chance it. He was still mad at Sam; Tommy wouldn't answer the letters his brother had been writing him, twice a week, since he left. But at the same time, he'd made a promise.

Tommy slunk into school and dropped the bag in his locker without incident. Unfortunately, once at his locker, he realized that actually stashing the tools inside the dead space would be harder than he thought. The bag was too big to just shove through the doggie door; he'd have to remove the tools and slide them through a few at a time.

That would be conspicuous and time-consuming.

Tommy milled around his locker for a while, hoping the hall would clear of students before the first bell rang, but it seemed like everyone was dragging this morning. The Wilmette kid, especially, was just standing around by his locker with a stupid, confused look on his face.

Frustrated, Tommy slammed his locker and marched to the bathroom, backpack once again on his shoulder. His only play would be to wait for first period to start, return to his locker, unload the tools, and then take a tardy.

LEFT BEHIND

Ernest Wilmette knew that bringing the art set to school was the thing he should do.

However, as soon as he opened his locker, Ernest grew anxious and confused. Maybe this whole thing had been a dumb idea. Maybe Ryan was right all along.

He was jolted from his thoughts by the loud, angry slam of a locker. He startled at the sound, but that was nothing compared to the sheer terror he felt when he looked up and saw Tommy Bricks barreling down the hallway with murder (or, at the very least, grave bodily injury) in his eyes.

The small part of Ernest's brain that wasn't presently consumed with his imminent annihilation couldn't help but wonder *why now?* Ernest and Tommy had both been at the lockers for a good five minutes, and Tommy hadn't seemed to notice. Perhaps, Ernest pondered, people like Tommy remembered rage the way someone like Ernest might remember to return a library book. *Oh, yeah. Silly me, I meant to beat the snot out of the Wilmette kid. Better get on that . . .*

But then, just at the moment when it was time for Ernest's life to start flashing before his eyes, Tommy marched right past him, down the hall, and around the corner.

Ernest noticed that Tommy's locker hadn't shut; he'd slammed it so hard the door had bounced back before the latch could catch. Not that it mattered. No one would dare steal from Tommy's locker.

Ernest's heartbeat had nearly returned to normal when the warning bell for first period rang. He quickly closed his locker and hurried to class . . . leaving the art set out on the floor at the foot of his locker.

TRUMAN THE CUSTODIAN

Truman the Custodian had been a fixture at Rod Serling Middle School for generations, not so much hired as installed, along with the lockers and drinking fountains. Extremely tall, extremely thin, and extremely old, he spent most of his day slowly pushing an industrial broom down the center of the halls while listening to NPR and big band music on the iPod his grandchildren had given him for Christmas. Whether the broom was actually collecting dust and debris or merely moving it from one end of the school to another remained open to debate.

In any case, that was precisely what Truman the Custodian was doing on this particular morning as his broom gathered and pushed Ernest's recently abandoned art set halfway down the hallway before the old janitor noticed it coasting along the floor at the end of his broom's soft bristles.

He stopped in front of Tommy's open locker and regarded the wooden box. Slowly, he bent down and picked up the art set, examining it briefly and with little interest. If Occam's razor is the theory that the simplest answer is usually the correct one, then Truman the Custodian's razor would state that the solution requiring the least effort was good enough for him. So Truman tossed the art set in the closest open locker before rising (again, slowly) and slamming the locker shut.

TOMMY FINDS THE ART SET

When Tommy returned to his locker ten minutes later, the hallway was empty. He opened his locker and crouched down to find his secret compartment. The back plate was cracked open an inch, which struck Tommy as odd. Maybe there was a draft in the dead space? He made a mental note to install a hook and latch to keep it closed in the future.

Tommy didn't notice the wooden box right away. When he loaded the tools in, he first reached as far as he could down into the shaft of dead space and then worked his way closer to center. So it was only after he'd loaded all of Sam's tools from the backpack that he discovered the art set.

Tommy took it out, confused. It looked like an old set. Maybe it had been sitting in the dead space behind the lockers for decades. Sam had worked construction all through high school and always came home with stories like that. Things getting lost during construction, things being discovered during demolition. Usually it was something you'd expect, a tool or lunch box or hard hat.

When you looked at it like that, a sixty-year-old art set hiding inside the hollow cavity of an old building wasn't such a stretch. Stranger things had happened.

And, besides, he'd always wanted an art set.

8

WHAT RYAN OVERLOOKED

Ryan couldn't concentrate on football. His head just wasn't in the game.

Yesterday, for reasons he still couldn't fathom, he had stood up to Tommy Bricks and Tommy had *let it slide*. For the rest of that evening and all this morning, Ryan had basked in the sunny glow, the exuberant thrill of being alive that only those who have just escaped certain death can fully appreciate. Colors looked brighter, food tasted better, and even a passing, pungent whiff from one of Declan's dirty diapers smelled oddly wonderful.

But Ryan was starting to realize that he had overlooked one tiny little detail. Just because Tommy wasn't holding a grudge against Ryan, that didn't mean he was done with Ernest Wilmette or Winston Patil.

This business was not necessarily over.

Ryan tried to focus on the game. Still, his gaze kept drifting back toward the picnic tables.

Where Tommy was now walking purposefully toward Winston with a fierce scowl on his face and a thick wooden box in his hands.

A LUNCHTIME SURPRISE

Ernest had no earthly clue what to do. He'd planned to use the art set to break the ice with Winston, but he didn't have the art set anymore, a realization he'd only just come to, on his way to lunch.

Winston sat at his usual table, alone, his head buried in his sketchbook. Ernest considered going up and talking to him anyway. But then he saw Tommy marching up to Winston's table with the wooden box under the crook of his arm. Ernest was confused. He had no idea how Tommy had got his hands on the art set or what he, Ernest, could do about it now.

Tommy reached Winston's table with an unreadable purpose. He looked kind of mad, but then he always looked that way.

Winston glanced up warily as Tommy slowly and deliberately lowered his arm, the art set gripped tightly in his fist.

At this point Ernest felt his stomach drop. That case was made of thick, heavy wood. Despite his best intentions, Ernest had given the most dangerous kid in school a big, box-shaped club.

"You see this?" It was Ryan, standing beside Ernest now.

Ernest nodded dumbly. Tommy's free hand rested on the table as he talked to Winston in a voice too low for them to hear.

"It's like I tried to tell you," Ryan said, leaving the but-you-wouldn't-listen part as understood. "You can't fix other people's problems. It just makes things worse. A kid like Tommy, he isn't going to stop—"

"Wait," Ernest said. "Look."

The boys watched, their jaws dropping in unison as Tommy rested the art set gently on the table, came around the side, and sat down next to Winston. Together, they opened the art set and began laying out the supplies on the table.

Ernest turned to Ryan.

"You were saying?"

HELP FROM THE WEIRD RICH KID

It had been a very strange morning, that was for sure. After lunch Tommy considered bringing the art set back to his locker, but he didn't want to part with it. Something about having it nearby made him feel . . . good.

"Wow," Mr. Earle said as he passed Tommy in the hallway between classes. "Now that is one serious set of art supplies." Tommy handed it over. Mr. Earle admired it. "Where'd you find one like this?"

It was an innocent question, but Tommy wasn't used to those. The questions Tommy was usually asked never presumed innocence. What Tommy heard was "Prove to me you didn't steal this."

"Um, I, uh—" Tommy stammered.

"He got it from me," a voice piped in from behind them. It was that Wilmette kid. "My aunt Tilly, she keeps sending me stuff like that, trying to make me an artist."

Tommy stared at the kid, unsure whether his luck had just improved or worsened.

"She's a bit off. Eighty-seven next January."

Worsened, Tommy decided quickly. The Wilmette kid was clearly new to lying, and like most amateurs, he was overdoing it.

"Still, I'm better off than my cousin Dudley. She thinks he's a . . ." The kid trailed off. He'd hit that wall, the moment when bad liars realize they've taken it all too far.

"We traded," Tommy cut in.

"Right," the Wilmette kid said, relieved. "I gave him the art set for a . . ."

"Baseball mitt."

"Yeah. A baseball mitt. Says David Ortega—"

"Ortiz."

"Ortiz. Right in the palm."

Mr. Earle said nothing through this muddled outpouring of information. He blinked for a moment, started to speak but then thought better of it, gave Tommy back his art set, and went on to his next class.

"Thanks," Tommy said to the Wilmette kid.

"No problem," the kid said, then went on his way as well.

"I didn't steal it," Tommy blurted out after him.

"I know," the kid called back, without turning around.

Tommy watched the kid walk down the hall. Something in the way the kid said that.

I know.

Like he really did know. For a fact.

Weird.

THE ODD FRIENDSHIP OF WINSTON PATIL AND TOMMY BRICKS

For the next week, Winston and Tommy spent lunch period together, sitting at the picnic table, eating and drawing. No one could believe it, not the kids, not the teachers—even Truman the Custodian took notice, and he routinely ignored the fire alarm.

At first the pairing was viewed with skepticism. But it was soon clear to everyone that these kids were, inexplicably but genuinely, becoming friends. Winston was undeniably happier at school, coming out of his shell little by little, both inside class and out. As for Tommy, he wasn't friendlier exactly, but the cold menace in his eyes did seem a tad less homicidal.

Under normal circumstances, the unlikely friendship of Winston Patil and Tommy Bricks would have been nothing more than a fleeting topic of conversation at Rod Serling Middle School. But on that fateful day when Winston went to Thompkins Well and humbly wished for a friend, two of his classmates, Aaron Robinette and Jamie Dahl, had spotted him from the nearby woods. Aaron was there looking for Bigfoot. Jamie was there to mock Aaron. Mr. Earle's discussion that day concerning the legend of the well was still fresh in the minds of the two boys, as was the barely averted lunchtime carnage when Tommy had harassed Winston over his drawings.

Aaron and Jamie naturally assumed that Winston had wished for Tommy to stop bullying him. So the fact that the very next day Tommy had not only stopped but had become his new best friend? That got kids talking.

Maybe Thompkins Well was more than a legend. Maybe it really was magic.

WHAT LIZZY WANTS

Lizzy MacComber did not believe in wishing wells. But you don't have to believe in wishes to make one. So after school, instead of going home, Lizzy went in the other direction, to North Side Park.

And Thompkins Well.

Her first thought was to wish for her dad to come back, but she discarded it almost as soon as she thought it. She could wish for him to come see her, maybe on the weekends sometimes. Lizzy's dad had moved to Columbus over the summer, and since then, Lizzy had only seen him once. They had talked on the phone a couple of times, and he always promised to stop by. But he never did.

Lizzy remembered reading a story about a monkey paw that granted wishes, but the wishes never worked out like they were supposed to. There was always a catch. At the end of the story, someone wishes for a dead person to come back to life, and the person comes back as a zombie. Somehow, Lizzie knew that's how it would be if she wished for her dad back. Unnatural and disappointing.

Now Lizzy was feeling silly for even thinking about any of this. Magic wells? Wishes? Zombies? It was all so absurd!

But that's not what was really eating at her. When a person considers what they would wish for, it can teach them a little something about themselves. Something a person may not want to learn.

Because when you hear people say something unkind about you enough times, even though you know it's not true, you still have a hard time not believing it.

Lizzy had a wish. She wasn't proud of it, but it was what she wanted.

9

MORE BABYSITTING FOR RYAN

Ryan was the only kid who didn't take any interest in the unlikely friendship between Winston and Tommy. He didn't buy into any of this magic well business. Sure, he'd heard the talk, how Aaron Robinette and Jamie Dahl had seen Winston at Thompkins Well the day before Winston and Tommy had become best buddies.

But Aaron believed in Bigfoot.

And Jamie was a meathead.

If anything, all it proved was that he and Ernest never should've butted in that day in the first place.

Ernest, however, had other ideas.

"No way," Ryan said. "We're not going back."

This was on a Wednesday, a week or so after their first visit to the well. They were outside the school, and Ryan was trying to walk home. Ernest was following.

"We have to," Ernest insisted.

"I am not taking you back to Thompkins Well."

Ryan started to walk away, but Ernest chased after him. "How can you say that? After everything that happened?"

"Everything that happened?" Ryan stopped and looked Ernest dead in the eye, to make sure he had his attention. "Ernest, *what happened* was that last week three kids—you, me, and Winston— all somehow escaped getting our butts kicked by the scariest guy in school. End of story. You do not press that kind of luck."

"C'mon, Ryan. You have to take me. I'll never find it by myself."

"Well, I guess that's that." Ryan brushed past, picking up his pace to signal he was done with the conversation.

"It wasn't luck," Ernest called after him. "At least, not entirely."

Ryan stopped. He didn't want to, he just . . . Man, why couldn't he get free of this kid?

Ernest scurried up to him and started talking a mile a minute. At first none of it made any sense. Something about a dirty attic and a dying grandfather and then this glowing old art set. It was like trying to listen to a four-year-old describe his dream to you. Then all this stuff about a feeling Ernest had. A feeling in his gut telling him to grab the art set and bring it to school and . . .

"Okay, slow down," Ryan said. "You're telling me this art set was *calling* to you in your dead grandfather's attic?"

"I wouldn't say *calling*," Ernest corrected with a thoughtful air of clarification. "More like it was very ready to be noticed."

"So you brought it to school and slipped it into Tommy's locker?"

"Yes. I mean, no. I brought it to school, but I didn't put it in Tommy's locker."

"Then how did he get his hands on it?"

"That's just it: I have no idea!" Ernest exclaimed, a slightly crazed, did-I-just-blow-your-mind-or-what gleam in his eyes.

"You know what? I don't care."

"What?" Ernest squealed in disbelief. "You cannot be serious!"

Ryan tried to walk past Ernest, but the smaller boy rushed awkwardly to block his path.

"Look, you were right," Ernest said quickly. "At the well. When I thought I could become Winston's friend and you said it doesn't work like that. You were right. I couldn't just *will* myself to be his friend. And I could never have *given* Tommy that art set. But that's why Tommy was picking on Winston in the first place. Winston's the best artist in the school, and Tommy—"

He didn't want to, but Ryan was starting to follow. "Tommy likes drawing, too."

"He wanted to learn."

It made sense. Still . . .

"Ryan, whatever happened, however that art set found its way to Tommy, it *worked*. Winston wished for a friend."

"And he got Tommy Bricks?"

"Well, I guess it does sound strange when you put it like that," Ernest conceded, but was quickly back at it again. "There's something going on here. Something special. Don't you think we should honor that? Help it along if we can?"

"No."

"Seriously?"

"I'm not taking you back to Thompkins Well, Ernest."

Ernest looked surprised at first, but then set his jaw and nodded. "Fine," he said with determination. "I'll go on my own."

Ernest turned and marched back toward the Nature Preserve.

Ryan watched as Ernest reached the tree line. He knew that Ernest would never find that cave by himself. At best he'd get lost for several hours, wandering around in circles and inching his way toward dehydration until the fire department found him. At worst he'd stumble upon some drunk high school kids who would smack him around and make him smoke menthol cigarettes until he threw up.

Ryan recalled a line from an old kung fu movie he saw with

his dad once, about how when you save a person's life, you then become responsible for that life. Ryan had never been sure what it meant, until now.

It meant that once you help someone out, they remain a pain in your butt forever.

DÉJÀ VU ALL OVER AGAIN

They had been sitting in the bottom of the well for almost half an hour. Ernest had taken off his windbreaker and was sitting on it to keep from getting his jeans wet.

So far it had been a bust. Shortly after they got there, a boy did come to make a wish. He even threw two quarters through the break in the slats for good measure.

But the kid was Aaron Robinette and he wished for Bigfoot, so Ernest figured that one didn't really count.

"I have to pee," Ernest announced, then felt foolish for sharing.

"Okay," Ryan said. "Go pee, then."

"Where?"

Ryan motioned down the cavern with his head. "What do you mean, where? Out."

"In the woods?"

"Well, you can't do it in here."

Ernest fidgeted. "Yeah, but . . . it just seems weird."

"Why?"

"I don't know. Out there in the woods, in the open. What if someone sees me?"

"That's stupid. If you stayed in here, someone would definitely see you."

"Well," Ernest considered. "Not if you left, and I stayed to—"

"Out, Ernest."

"Fine." He sulked out of the cavern to pee in the woods.

ALONE IN THE WELL

It was quiet for a few moments. Then Ryan heard someone up above.

"Okay, first off," came a girl's voice from the top of the well, "I don't believe in miracles or magic or fairy tales and I especially don't believe in Prince Charming, because even in the best circumstances, being a princess stinks. You can't do anything you want. Living life in a castle, you might as well be a prisoner. And being subjugated is no way to live. So we're clear."

Subjugated? Ryan only knew two people who talked like that. Mr. Earle and . . .

"And I'm sure there's a logical, reasonable explanation for why Tommy and Winston became friends."

Lizzy MacComber. The penny dropped then, literally, as Lizzy threw down a coin, pegging Ryan on the forehead.

"Ouch," he muttered, rubbing his head.

"Anyway, if there really is anything to all this wishing and magic stuff, and I still don't think there is, to be perfectly honest, then I'd want . . ."

Ryan could hear the frustration in her voice. Whatever she wanted, she didn't want to say it.

"Sometimes I feel like this dorky weirdo who reads too much and thinks too much and can't carry on a simple conversation," Lizzy blurted out. Then she added quietly, "I just . . . I wish I knew how to be pretty."

Ryan heard some faint rustling and shifting of feet, like she had walked away and then changed her mind.

"That's what I would wish for," Lizzy said, with a little punch behind her voice. "If I believed in these kinds of things. Which, again, I don't. Just so we're clear." ·

There was silence after that. She had left.

Ryan heard Ernest coming back through the cavern. He ducked into the tunnel and hurried to catch Ernest before he reached the well.

"Come on," Ryan said, ushering Ernest to the entrance. "We're done with this."

"Okay," Ernest said amiably as Ryan led them out of the narrow cavern. "Probably ought to call it a day, yeah?"

"Yeah, yeah," Ryan said, looking back at the cavern entrance.

"You know, I've been thinking," Ernest said as they stared at the trail. "Last time I went to my grandfather's attic first, and then I came here. Maybe that's what I should have done."

"Sure," Ryan said. "'Cause who knows? Maybe your grandpa's had Bigfoot in his attic all this time."

"You're making fun of me," Ernest said, but he was smiling, like he knew something Ryan didn't.

"Let's just get moving." They started down the trail, then Ernest stopped.

"Hold up," he said.

"What now?"

"I left my windbreaker."

Ernest shrugged sheepishly, then ran back into the cavern while Ryan waited, impatiently, outside.

PAIGE BARNETT

Ernest found his windbreaker right where he'd left it. But as he grabbed it, he heard a girl's voice overhead.

"Hello?" It sounded familiar. "Um, my name is Paige. Paige Barnett."

Paige Barnett? Ernest stood frozen in the center of the well, clutching his damp windbreaker in his fist, afraid to make the slightest sound.

"I'm not . . . I'm not here for me," she said, her voice a little shaky. "It's my little brother, Seth. He's in first grade and he's having a hard time reading. A really hard time. And it doesn't make any sense. He's a smart kid, he really is, but he just can't seem to . . ."

Her voice got shakier and trailed off. Ernest was surprised. Paige was pretty and popular, the kind of kid who seemed to have it easy. But this was clearly something that had been weighing on her mind.

"I don't know what to do. My parents don't, either. The teachers . . . Everyone's trying but nothing's working. Seth is miserable. He cries a lot. He tries to hide it, but I hear him in his room," she said, fighting back tears herself. "And I wish I knew how to help."

Once back outside with Ryan, Ernest told him about Paige Barnett and her little brother.

"That settles it," Ryan said adamantly.

"Absolutely," Ernest concurred wholeheartedly.

"That's the last time we go in that well."

"I completely agr—wait. No."

"We have no right to be hearing this stuff."

"We can help. We have a responsibility to help."

"We can't help. And we have a responsibility to mind our own stinking business."

Ernest wanted to disagree, but there was a part of Paige's wish he hadn't shared with Ryan. Paige had proposed a deal, a bargain.

"Mr. Earle told us about the legend," Paige had said. "About how Ezekiel Thompkins offered his life in exchange for his grandson's. So, I figure that's how it must work; wishes cost, right? Well, I'm pretty smart. Maybe not Lizzy MacComber smart, but I get good grades and all that. So, I'm thinking I can give some of my smarts to my little brother, to help him. To even things out a bit. That sounds fair, doesn't it?"

It was an honest bargain. Whether she believed the well had the power to pull it off or not, Ernest could hear in Paige's voice that she had meant what she said. She'd do anything to help her little brother.

That really stuck with Ernest, but it also kind of proved Ryan's point. Ernest did feel wrong listening to Paige like that.

All the more reason, he decided, to make it mean something.

"Tomorrow I'm going into my grandfather's attic," Ernest announced with renewed gumption. "You'll see—it'll be just like what happened with Winston and Tommy."

"Sounds great. You do that."

Ernest nodded, overlooking Ryan's sarcasm. "So I'll just tell my mom I'm coming home with you after school?"

"Tell your mom whatever you—what? No."

"C'mon."

"No. You cannot come home with me."

"But—"

"Listen, I'm done babysitting you, all right?"

Ernest stopped, stung. "O-okay," he said quietly.

"Look, don't—all right, whatever," Ryan said with an irritated groan. "You can walk home with me, but that's it. I have things I have to do." Tomorrow was Thursday, grocery day with Mrs. Haemmerle.

Ernest brightened. "That's fine. I'll search the attic while you're doing your things. We can meet up later. It's perfect."

"Yeah," Ryan said. "Perfect."

10

ERNEST RETURNS TO THE ATTIC

Ernest walked home with Ryan the following day. Though he had driven through the South Side dozens of times when Grandpa Eddie was still alive, walking through Ryan's neighborhood now felt different, like he was someplace new and unfamiliar.

As Ernest had suspected, Ryan didn't seem any more excited about Ernest's plan than he had the day before. He didn't talk much along the way, and his antsy pace told Ernest to "come on and get this over with already."

When they got to Grandpa Eddie's house, Ryan stopped at the curb. "You have a way inside?"

Ernest nodded. Grandpa Eddie had kept a spare house key hidden under a rock in the back garden.

"All right, then," Ryan said, and walked across the street, leaving Ernest to it.

Ernest keyed his way in through the back door. As he stepped inside he felt like he was burgling the old house. It felt kind of cool—that is, until he got to the attic. The farther he made his way in between the dusty piles of boxes and stacks of luggage, the more he started to suspect that he really knew very little about his grandfather. He and Grandpa Eddie had been close; at least, Ernest had thought so. But there was so much stuff in this attic, and he had no idea what any of it really meant.

Like the art set. At the time, Ernest hadn't thought that much about what a sixty-year-old art set, brand-new and in perfect condition, was doing on a rocking chair with all those other old, unopened toys. It didn't make any sense, though. Who would buy a bunch of toys and then just stick them all in an attic for more than half a century?

What Ernest did know was that Grandpa Eddie wanted him up here, that he was meant to find these toys. He went through the pile, taking all the items off the seat of the rocking chair and laying them out slowly, carefully. There were five in all:

A box of Colorforms

A sock monkey

A Flash Gordon click ray pistol

A handmade quilt

A fire extinguisher

The last two weren't toys. The quilt, however, was something you could give to a child. Maybe that was it—they were gifts. But gifts for who?

Or, perhaps just as importantly, gifts for when?

And that still didn't explain the old-timey fire extinguisher. No matter how he looked at it, Ernest couldn't see how it fit in with the others.

He glanced around the room. If only some sign would come to him, some inspiration like he'd gotten with the art set, then he'd know what to do next. So far, however, he was getting nothing. Last time, he didn't really have a chance to think about it. He saw the art set and knew he had to take it with him.

This time nothing jumped out at him. He tried to use reason. He thought about Paige Barnett and her wish. She wanted her little brother to read, but none of these toys would help with that. There weren't any books in the pile, nothing that had any educational application that Ernest could think of.

He opened the box of old Colorforms. Inside was a series of small vinyl pieces, different sizes and shapes that pressed on and peeled off a laminated play board. A nice enough toy, but Ernest didn't see how it could help. Still, the box had been stacked under the art set, with the fire extinguisher and ray gun behind and the quilt draped over the back. It stood to reason that it would be next in line; everything else was clearly behind it. He grabbed the Colorforms box and left the attic before he could second-guess himself.

THE NEW NEIGHBOR BOY

When they got back from the supermarket, Ryan brought the groceries into the house and stacked them in the cupboards. Then Mrs. Haemmerle sent him out to the front porch while she put together a tray of shortbread cookies and some lemonade.

It was a ritual of sorts. After groceries they'd sit together on her front porch and drink the lemonade. Sometimes they'd talk a bit. For an old lady, she stayed pretty current on TV and movies and music.

Today, though, they were both kind of quiet. That was fine, too. Sometimes just sitting was nice.

Then Mrs. Haemmerle leaned forward in her chair and started looking across the street. "Huh," she said, squinting into the sun a bit. "Looks like a family has moved into Eddie Wilmette's old house." She pointed discreetly across the street.

"What?" Ryan garbled, almost spitting out a mouthful of lemonade.

"There's a boy watching us from across the front yard." She screwed up her face. "Strange. I didn't even know they put the house on the market."

It took Ryan a moment to piece it together. He'd forgotten all about Ernest, who was now standing motionless in the middle of his grandfather's front lawn like a confused garden gnome.

"No, Mrs. Haemmerle, that's not—"

"I'll get another glass," she said, already rising from her chair. "Go invite that boy over for some lemonade, Ryan. We can welcome him to the neighborhood."

"But he's not new," Ryan started. It was no use. Mrs. Haemmerle could be surprisingly spry at times and was already back inside the house.

Ryan walked across the street. "What are you doing?" he asked when he got closer to Ernest.

Ernest shrugged, a bit sheepish. "I don't know. I finished in the attic and . . ."

Ryan was getting so he could tell when Ernest had another shoe to drop. "And what?" he growled with a tired sigh.

"When I told my mom I was coming home with you, she said to call from your house when I wanted her to come get me."

"Come on." Ryan started walking back across the street.

"Are we going back to your house now?"

"No," Ryan said. "First you have to have some lemonade. And meet the neighbors."

A FAMILIAR FACE

Ernest followed Ryan to the house across the street. The old lady Ryan was drinking lemonade with before had come back out with a fresh glass and was pouring when Ernest and Ryan reached the porch.

When the old lady saw Ernest, her face suddenly drained of color; she looked like she'd just seen a ghost.

"Mrs. Haemmerle," Ryan said, not noticing how shook up the old lady was. "This is Ernest Wilmette. Mr. Wilmette's grandson. He's in my class at school."

The color returned to Mrs. Haemmerle's face, but she still kept staring at Ernest. Then she shook it off and laughed at herself. "I'm so sorry. Ernest, is it? Please forgive me for staring. But, my word, you look just like him."

ROLLO, REVEALED

The boys sat on the porch while Mrs. Haemmerle hurried inside to find something. Ryan looked at Ernest quizzically.

"What?" Ernest said defensively. "I didn't do anything."

Mrs. Haemmerle returned with an old photo album, flipping

through the pages as she sat down. "Aha," she said as she took a really old photo out of the album and handed it to Ernest.

It was black and white and very brittle. Three kids, two boys and a girl in the middle, were eating ice cream on some porch steps. The first boy looked older, maybe fourteen, while the other boy and the girl were younger, maybe nine or ten.

"Holy—what?" Ryan said, peering over Ernest's shoulder. "That's you!"

The younger boy was a dead ringer for Ernest, no doubt about it. No wonder Mrs. Haemmerle nearly lost it.

"That's me in the middle," she said, leaning over and nodding her head. "Your grandfather is the older boy on the left. That picture was taken on those steps, right over there," she said, pointing to Grandpa Eddie's porch.

Ernest looked over at the house, then back at the picture. "Then who is this?" he said, pointing to his doppelganger.

Mrs. Haemmerle smiled sadly. "That's Robert," she said. Saying the name made her eyes tear up. "He was your great-uncle. Or he would've been. He died a month after that picture was taken."

Ernest couldn't believe it. No one had told him about any of this before. "Grandpa Eddie had a brother?"

Mrs. Haemmerle nodded. "Oh, yes. Robert was the sweetest boy I ever . . ." She trailed off, fighting tears now.

"How . . . how did he die?" Ryan asked quietly.

Mrs. Haemmerle collected herself. "He had what they called an oversized heart. It's the kind of condition that's very treatable today, but back then . . . Anyway, one day, his heart just got too big. He went to sleep and never woke up."

Ernest looked at the image again. Knowing now, it was easy to see Grandpa Eddie and Mrs. Haemmerle in the picture. As for Robert, all Ernest saw was himself. It just didn't seem real.

He numbly handed the photo back to Mrs. Haemmerle. She held it up to the light for one last, close look before putting it away in the album. As she did, Ernest glimpsed some writing on the back of the picture.

"Excuse me, Mrs. Haemmerle?" Ernest said, holding out his hand. "May I take another look?"

"Oh, certainly, dear." She handed it to him. He flipped it over to read the back.

Eddie   **Me**   **Rollo**

Rollo . . .

"You called him Rollo?"

Mrs. Haemmerle chuckled. "I called him Robert. Everyone else called him Rollo. Your grandfather gave him that nickname. He was a very plump baby."

THE MOMS

Ryan brought Ernest back to his house. If Ryan's mom was surprised that he'd brought home the boss's son, she didn't show it. Ernest called his mom, who said she'd be over in twenty minutes.

Ryan felt self-conscious having Ernest in his home. He knew Ernest's house—everyone did. It was the nicest house in town. He kept waiting for Ernest to give himself away, to make some kind of face, however subtly, that showed he was looking down on Ryan and his family and how they lived.

But Ernest never did. In fact, Ernest spent the twenty minutes chatting with Ryan's mom.

Mrs. Wilmette arrived and Ryan's mom invited her inside. Ryan expected Mrs. Wilmette to defer, to snatch up Ernest and whisk him back to the North Side, pronto. But she didn't. She came right in, and before Ryan knew it the two women were sitting at the kitchen table drinking iced tea.

Mrs. Wilmette went right for Declan. Ryan watched as his little brother immediately got applesauce all over Mrs. Wilmette's cashmere sweater. He waited for the conversation to turn awkward and terse, to hear words like *expensive* and *dry cleaning* and *grubby little hands*, but Mrs. Wilmette could not have cared less about the stains. Declan could've puked in her face and she probably would have laughed it off.

The two moms quickly fell into easy conversation. After about five minutes, Ryan led Ernest into the den.

"Your mom's cool," Ryan said.

Ernest nodded. "She loves kids," he said. "She wanted a big family, but there were complications with me. And now she can't have any more."

Ryan was taken aback by Ernest's bluntness.

"Shocking, I know," Ernest said, as if reading Ryan's mind. "Me and complications."

Ryan looked at him. He thought about joking back, but it didn't seem right. "So, did you find something in the attic?"

"I think so," Ernest said, brightening. "We'll see."

11

FLYING BLIND WITH COLORFORMS

The next day, Ernest brought the Colorforms set to school in his backpack. He still had no idea how colored vinyl shapes were going to help a little boy learn to read, but he refused to entertain the thought that they would aid in the discovery of Bigfoot. Then again, he never could have imagined the impact an art set would have had on Tommy Bricks and Winston Patil. All day long, he tried to figure out what he should do with them, but nothing seemed right.

By the end of the day the Colorforms were still in his backpack. On the plus side, the box was light and made of soft cardboard, so it was easy for Ernest to forget it was even there.

After school, Ryan had to babysit his little brother, so Ernest just went home. When he got to the house, his mom had left him a note saying she'd gone out and could he return some library books for her. The books were on the kitchen counter next to the note. Ernest dumped his schoolbooks out of his backpack and replaced them with the library books.

On the way to the library, Ernest started thinking about the picture Mrs. Haemmerle had shown him yesterday. Ordinarily, the overwhelming resemblance between him and Rollo would be a lot to take in, but it was nothing compared to finding out that he'd had an uncle he'd never even known about.

Ernest looked just like Rollo. How could that have never come up? Not once? How could Grandpa Eddie have kept that from him all these years?

It made Ernest angry, the more he thought about it.

But more than angry, it made him feel alone.

OOPS

Despite himself, Ryan was warming up to Ernest. But the kid was a lot to take. So when Ryan's mom had asked him to come home early from school to watch Declan, he was actually excited to just walk home by himself without having to worry about Ernest or Tommy or anyone else bothering him.

"Hey, Ryan." Lizzy hurried to catch up with him. "Haven't seen you around much lately."

Ryan deflated. "Oh, hey, Lizzy." He used to like talking to Lizzy, but ever since that weird thing with the magazines, he wasn't sure what her deal was anymore.

"Wanna walk home together?"

"I guess."

Lizzy winced. "You guess?"

"Yeah," he said. "Sure."

She stopped walking. "Don't do me any favors, Hardy."

Like this. Exactly like this.

"What are you—I'm not . . ."

"*I guess,*" Lizzy said, making her voice sound thick and stupid.

Ryan said, "Why are you being such a jerk?"

"Why are you so stuck-up all the time?"

"I'm not stuck-up—"

"Every time I try to talk to you, you look at me like I'm some three-headed alien."

"I do not. I just don't want to talk about girls in magazines."

Lizzy's eyes teared up a little. "Fine! Forget it," she shouted, and then started walking quickly ahead of him. Ryan felt bad, then frustrated. It's just like with Ernest, he thought. They push so hard, then when you finally push back, you're the one who's a jerk.

"I just can't win," Ryan muttered to himself. "Lizzy!" he called after her. "Lizzy, stop!"

She didn't stop.

"You *are* pretty!" he yelled. He said it before he even thought it. The words just jumped out of his mouth.

Lizzy stopped immediately. She turned around. "What did you say?"

"I said, you are pretty. And I don't get why you think you're not."

DROP BOX

Out in front of the library was a brick book-deposit box a little bigger than a trash can, with a huge rolling door you pulled down from the top. Ernest yanked the handle with one hand and grabbed the books from his backpack with the other.

There's a special moment that everyone experiences from time to time. A brief instant when you realize, too late to stop it, that you're in the process of making a really stupid mistake. Like when you accidentally let a door lock behind you, or knock your toothbrush off the edge of the sink and into the toilet.

Ernest experienced one of those special moments as he closed the rolling door on the book-deposit box and realized that in addition to his mother's library books, he'd dropped the Colorforms set inside as well.

Frustrated, Ernest went to the library entrance. But the library was closed early for inventory, and it would be closed all weekend, too. The soonest he could come back would be Monday, after school.

It was like what had happened with the art set all over again.

RYAN AND HIS BIG MOUTH

"Ow! Seriously, Lizzy!" Ryan said, holding the bridge of his nose, where Lizzy had just socked him. Hard.

"How do you know?"

"What?"

"Don't 'what' me, Ryan Hardy," she seethed. "You heard me. You were at Thompkins Well."

The pain in Ryan's nose disappeared, replaced by a queasy one in his stomach. Because it wasn't until that moment that he realized, fully, what he had just said to Lizzy. He hadn't just called her pretty.

"You *are* pretty" was what he'd said, as if he were responding to an earlier statement. Which, of course, he was.

And if that weren't bad enough, he'd sealed it by saying he didn't understand why she didn't think she was pretty, too. He couldn't believe it. He'd always heard that girls could make a guy stupid, but he never understood how until this moment.

"Okay," Ryan said, figuring the truth was his only option. "Yes, I did hear you."

"But I never saw you at the park." She looked at him with growing suspicion. "Were you spying on me?"

"It's not like that," he said quickly.

"Then what is it like?" she spat.

It was a perfectly straightforward question. The answer, unfortunately, wouldn't be.

"I wasn't at Thompkins Well," Ryan said. "I was . . . in Thompkins Well."

Ten minutes later and all Lizzy said was "So. Monday, then?"

"What?"

Ryan had told her everything as quickly and succinctly as he could. It had felt good to get it all out, but the more he talked, the more ridiculous the whole thing sounded. When he mentioned how Ernest thought his late grandfather's attic was magically telling him to give things to people, he'd been sure she was going to pop him in the nose again.

But she hadn't. In fact, the stranger the story got, the more Lizzy seemed to loosen up. When Ryan got to the part about Aaron Robinette asking the well to help him find Bigfoot, she'd actually laughed.

Then she hit him with this business about a private tour.

"You heard me, Hardy," she said. "Monday, after school, you're taking me inside the well."

"But I thought you believed me."

"Oh, I do. You could never have made up a story that good."

Ryan wasn't sure how to take that.

"Still," Lizzy said, "I want to see it for myself."

FAMILY SECRETS

Once he learned about Rollo, Ernest began to notice the way his parents often talked in a kind of conversational shorthand—key words and phrases that for them made perfect sense but that he, Ernest, could not possibly decipher.

Like tonight, at dinner.

"I'm set with Bilkes for Tuesday," his dad said, looking down at his chicken.

"Oh," his mom said, trying to sound nonchalant. "Is that fast?"

"Yes and no," his dad said. He looked up then. "It's still early in the process. Doesn't mean anything, one way or the other."

Wow, right in front of him. How many of these coded conversations had he missed? It was like a whole world opening up to him.

Except it wasn't. Because Ernest still didn't have a clue what they were talking about. He didn't even know who Bilkes was. All he knew for sure was that the discussion sounded serious and that they didn't want him to know about it. Maybe it had to do with all the late nights his dad was putting in at the factory, and at home.

"I met Karen Hardy yesterday," his mom said.

"Really?"

"Ernest went over there, to hang out with Ryan."

His dad practically did a double take. Ernest didn't *hang out* with other kids much. He was liked well enough at school, but he didn't have what you'd call, well, friends.

"Doug Hardy's been working with me a lot on this deal. I'm going to put him in charge of the account if . . ." His dad trailed off.

Ernest's mom turned her attention to him. "Anyway," she said, "maybe next time you can invite Ryan over here."

Or I can just tell myself to get lost and save Ryan the trouble, thought Ernest.

"Sure, Mom" was what he said, though.

Ernest was itching to say something about meeting Mrs. Haemmerle, maybe even tell them about the picture of Grandpa Eddie and Rollo. Or maybe he could start a coded conversation of his own, something he could say that they would have to wonder about.

So after he finished dinner, he said to his parents: "I've got some homework to do still. Best I just *rollo* on up and out of here."

His dad gave him nothing.

"Okay, honey. Clear your plate," said his mom.

Well, it still felt good to say Rollo's name out loud, anyway.

NO WAY AROUND IT

On Monday at lunch, Ryan told Ernest to show Lizzy what he'd taken from his grandfather's attic.

"I can't," Ernest said.

"What do you mean, you can't?" Ryan said. "Just show her. It's okay. I told her everything."

"Really?" Ernest's face lit up. "And she bought it?" He looked at Lizzy eagerly. She fluttered her hand in a jury's-still-out kind of way.

"That's why I want you to show her what you took from your grandfather's attic."

"Oh, forget that. It was a box of Colorforms, but I accidentally dropped it in the library's book-return box."

"You did what?" Ryan said.

"Doesn't matter. We should really show her the well anyway."

"Yeah, I was hoping we wouldn't have to—"

But Ernest had already turned to Lizzy. "It's so cool. You have to crouch through this low, narrow tunnel. That part's a little spooky, but there's really nothing to it."

Lizzy laughed. "Sounds like fun," she said.

"Sure, loads of fun," Ryan said.

A FEW WORDS ABOUT HOME FINANCE

After the last bell, Lizzy followed Ryan and Ernest into the woods behind the school.

"Now, they say there's a devil-worshipping cult that practices in these woods," Ernest said with an air of authority. "But don't worry, it's just a story the high school kids tell to scare people away so they can misbehave in peace."

Lizzy liked Ernest. He was very sweet and funny, too. The kid said *misbehave*, for Pete's sake.

Ryan went into the cave first. Lizzy followed him, and then Ernest. When they got to the bottom of the well, Ernest tapped her on the shoulder. "Isn't it amazing?" he said.

Amazing wasn't the word she would have used, but it was pretty cool.

"Okay," Ryan said abruptly. "You've seen the well. Let's go."

"What?" Ernest protested. "We can't go now. We have to wait and see if anyone comes to make a wish."

"No, we don't."

"Sure we do," Ernest said. "It's the only way to really prove to Lizzy that you heard her from down here, that you're telling the truth. Right?" He looked at Lizzy for that last part, giving her a mischievous smile.

They didn't have to wait long. About ten minutes later, they heard footsteps approaching.

"Hey, Mr. Well," a boy's voice began. "It's me, Aaron Robinette, again. I figured the last time I might not have made my wish very clearly. I wasn't asking *for* Bigfoot, like to have one of my own. Because, like, that would be stupid. It's just that my friend Jamie, he keeps making fun of me because I believe in Bigfoot. Right? Anyway, he's kind of a jerk about it, and I'd just like to shut him up, you know? Just a little proof would be nice, to shut up Jamie. My friend. The jerk. Anyway, thanks."

They heard Aaron shuffle away.

Ryan shook his head in wonder. "Mr. Well?"

Lizzy countered, "I thought it was kind of sweet—"

"Hold on," Ernest interrupted. "I think I hear someone else."

"Um. Hello?" It was a boy again, but a different one this time. Lizzy didn't recognize the voice, but it sounded older. In high school, maybe.

Ernest gave her an eager thumbs-up while Ryan set his jaw and looked away.

The boy at the well threw down a quarter. Then he started talking about his dad, who worked construction. He'd been having back problems. Their insurance wouldn't cover a specialist and money was tight, so his dad had to cut back on the jobs he could take. Roofing paid the best but was hardest on his body, so he had to start taking drywall jobs.

The boy's mom worked as a bank teller, and her hours were getting squeezed. They were still getting by, but just barely. As Lizzy listened, she was struck by the way the boy never complained as he told his story. He worked afternoons as a stock boy for a local supermarket, and on the weekends he baled hay for a farmer out in the country. In fact, he was at the well because he was wishing for extra work.

Because on top of everything else, the boy's grandmother, his mom's mom, was sick in Boston and probably wasn't going to make it much longer. His folks were trying to fly his mom out to visit, to say goodbye, really, but the flights were so expensive. The boy hoped, if he could just earn a little more here and there, they could fly his mom to Boston without getting behind on the house.

"What did he mean?" Ernest asked after the boy had left. "That part about getting behind on the house."

"He was talking about their mortgage," Ryan said. "Do you know what a mortgage is?"

Ernest nodded. "It's a loan families get so they can buy a house. The bank gives you the money to buy the house and you pay them back a little each month until you've paid it all back."

Ryan said, "Getting behind is when you start missing your monthly payments. Miss a few of them and the bank takes your house away."

"They can do that?"

"Of course they can," Ryan said. "Until you pay them back, they own the house."

"So," Lizzy cut in. "Do you guys think you can help him?"

"No, we can't help him," Ryan said flatly. "I don't know what happened with Winston and Tommy, but it wasn't because of some magic attic. This is exactly why I didn't want to come here anymore. We shouldn't be hearing this stuff."

"But maybe we can—" Ernest began.

"Stop it. We can't." Ryan straightened and brushed the dirt off his jeans. "Don't you get it? That kid just wanted to get his problems off his chest for a minute. That's all. He doesn't want to whine to his parents or his friends, but it's a lot to keep inside, so he talks to a big hole in the ground."

With that, Ryan left the well. Lizzy and Ernest followed. No one talked as they walked out of the woods. Ryan's words had clearly stung Ernest, but it was hard to keep that kid down for long.

"Don't worry about him," Ernest said as he tugged lightly on Lizzy's arm. "He's coming around."

"Ernest," Lizzy said. "Do you really believe..." She didn't know how to finish the sentence. "All of this?"

"Of course," he said with the kind of unflinching faith usually reserved for the delusional. "Don't you?"

Lizzy looked at him. His eyes were big and hopeful.

"I don't know," she said.

Ernest clapped his hands. "That's good enough for me!"

12

CONVERGENCE INSUFFICIENCY

Jenny Davenport loved books. But after four hours of sorting and stacking and stamping, even she could get kind of sick of them.

Jenny was a junior at the high school. Three days a week she volunteered at the library, usually only for a couple of hours here and there. But this week Mrs. Conway, the librarian, was doing inventory. So she really needed Jenny to help with the day-to-day stuff, like checking out books at the counter, sending overdue emails, and collecting the returned books from the curbside depository.

And to top it all off, Mrs. Conway's son, Jason, was constantly in the way. He really couldn't help it: He was five, hopped up on sugar, and bored—an unstoppable triple-threat of annoying. At least the library was closed now, so she didn't have to worry about him running around and bothering the patrons.

Jenny just wanted to finish her shift, get home, grab some dinner, and start her homework. She had a paper due for her biology class. Every week, Mr. Broderick made them write a short paper on some random, science-related topic. This week, they had to write about an obscure physical ailment. She was not looking forward to it.

"Whatcha doing?" Jason was suddenly at her side behind the counter, leaning into her personal space and breathing his hot Doritos breath into her neck.

Jenny sighed. "You know what I'm doing, Jason." The boy had moved on, though, and was now digging through the returned books Jenny had just brought in from the curbside depository.

"Hey, what's this?" He started tugging at something in the middle of the stack.

"Jason, stop it. The books are going to—"

Too late. The stack toppled off the counter and onto the floor.

"Great. Just great." Jenny wheeled around the counter toward the fallen books. Jason, agitated, bent down to start picking them up. "Just leave them. I'll do it," Jenny snapped.

Jason stepped back, trembling. She knew it was an accident.

The kid didn't mean it. She looked to the floor and saw what he'd been grabbing at: an old box of Colorforms. She picked it up. "Is this what you were looking at?"

Jason nodded warily. Jenny examined the box. It was really old, but in good shape. What would something like this be doing in the book depository? Sometimes people used the depository to donate old books, but this was a toy. It was strange, very strange, but it was also exactly what Jenny needed right now.

She held the box up to Jason. "Think you can take this to the table and play quietly for a while?"

Jason nodded, brightening instantly. She handed him the box and he ran off.

True to his word, the boy was playing quietly at a nearby table by the time Jenny finished picking up the last of the fallen books. It was facedown on the floor and when she turned it over, an open page caught her eye.

Convergence Insufficiency, it said at the top.

She checked the cover. It was some kind of medical book. She went back and skimmed the page. Apparently, convergence insufficiency was a vision problem where your eyes wouldn't work together whenever you tried to read. It was like one eye was looking at one part of the page while the other eye was looking at another part.

A voracious reader herself, Jenny couldn't imagine having a physical ailment like that. An obscure physical ailment . . .

Jenny logged the book into the computer and then checked it out herself and put it in her backpack. She had a topic for her science paper at least.

COUNCIL GETS REAL

It rained most of that week, and though that meant Ryan couldn't play football at lunch, at least the rain kept Ernest from dragging him to that stupid well.

Unfortunately, Ernest used the downtime to work on Lizzy, winning her over to his side of things. Ryan wasn't sure Lizzy really bought it, at least not a hundred percent, but all you had to do was see Winston Patil and Tommy Bricks sitting at the picnic tables together, or staring into the courtyard and muttering to each other, and even a cynic like Ryan had to wonder. At least a little.

In fact, just this morning Ryan had seen Winston and Tommy talking to Mr. Earle after class. Ryan's first guess was that the honeymoon was over and Winston was telling on Tommy, but it was clear from the way they huddled near one another that they had come to the teacher together. And whatever they were saying had Mr. Earle interested.

Later in the day, Mr. Earle opened up Council by asking the

class if anyone had something they wanted to talk about. Paige Barnett immediately raised her hand.

Everyone, even Mr. Earle, looked surprised.

"Okay, Paige," he said. "Please, what's on your mind?"

Paige stood up. She looked excited and a little nervous. "My younger brother, Seth, he's in first grade. And he's been having a really, really tough time learning to read. It's been hard on everyone, hard on my parents, hard on Seth for sure."

"And hard on you," Mr. Earle said quietly.

Paige nodded. "But then, Seth's teacher, she found out about this condition where your eyes don't work together when you try to read. So we had Seth's vision tested and now we know what the problem is. And the best part is that it's completely fixable. Seth has to wear these funny glasses to read now, and it's going to take a long time to get right, but he's reading. He's really reading."

With unflinching resolve, Ryan looked straight ahead. But out of the corner of his eye, he could see Ernest bouncing in his chair like a panicked toddler about to lose a battle with his bladder. Ryan finally gave in and glanced over at Ernest, who cupped the sides of his face with his hands while mouthing to Ryan slowly and deliberately: "SHE. WAS. AT. THE. WELL."

Ryan gave him a sharp look back that loosely translated to *I know, idiot. I was there with you.*

"Wow," said Mr. Earle, amazed. "How did this teacher figure out Seth's problem?"

"That's the neatest part, Mr. Earle," Paige said. "Seth's teacher's boyfriend is a high school science teacher, and one of his students wrote a paper about it."

Ryan tried to look on the bright side. This time, at least, it was more of a stretch to think they had anything to do with Paige's wish coming true. Unlike with Winston and Tommy, there was no magic art set that made it happen. No smoking gun, as the expression goes. A high school girl's homework had helped Paige's brother learn to read, not some stupid box of Colorforms.

"That's a wonderful coincidence," Mr. Earle said.

"I know, right," Paige said. "It's actually a funny story. My parents met with the science teacher and his student, to thank them, you know. And the girl who wrote the paper, she said she only even discovered the eye condition because it was in this medical textbook the librarian's son had knocked over trying to get at this box of . . . I forget what she called them. They're like stickers but they're plastic and you can reuse them?"

"Colorforms?" Mr. Earle said, surprised.

"That's it," Paige said.

Ryan heard Ernest across the room, squeaking.

"My word. Colorforms," Mr. Earle chuckled. "Do they even make those anymore?"

"I don't know. This one was a really old set. Like an antique or something."

Another squeak, this one longer and higher pitched, like Ernest was a balloon losing air.

"Anyway, someone had left these Colorforms in the library, I guess. So, as she went to pick up the book, she found it face-down on the floor and open to the page that talked about my brother's eye problem. And she wrote her paper about it. Isn't that weird?"

"That," said Mr. Earle slowly, "just might be the most remarkable thing I've ever heard."

Ryan struggled gamely to look for a bright side. At least, he thought, she didn't mention going to Thompkins Well.

"I know," said Paige. "I guess that well really is magic."

Nuts.

"Come again?" Mr. Earle said.

"Oh, right," Paige said. "Whoops! I left that part out. What do you call that, when you tell a story and forget the most important part?"

"I think 'burying the lede' is the expression you're looking for."

"Right. So two weeks ago I went to Thompkins Well. I remembered the story you told in class, Mr. Earle, and figured it couldn't hurt."

"You wished for your brother to be able to read?"

Please, please don't say it, Ryan thought.

"Uh-huh. And now he's reading!"

Ryan's head dropped onto his desk as the class erupted in excited chatter.

SHUT UP, ERNEST

"Magic. Magic, magic, magic!"

"Shut up, Ernest."

But Ernest was far too excited to shut up.

"Ryan," Lizzy admonished.

"Oh, he's fine," Ernest said blithely as he danced around them in victory, singing, "Magic, magic, magic!" like a one-person conga line.

"Will you stop that!"

Ernest did. "Sorry," he said. "But you gotta admit this is all too much to be a coincidence."

Ryan took a loud breath through his nose. "Maybe," he said doubtfully.

"Yes!" Ernest exclaimed. "I knew you'd come around."

"Maybe," Ryan continued. "Maybe there is something . . ."

"Magical," Ernest coaxed. "Say *magical*."

"Unexplainable—"

"Really?"

"—going on here. But whatever it is, thinking we're a part of it is still a stretch."

"A stretch? A stretch?!" Ernest couldn't believe this guy.

"He's right, Ryan," Lizzy said. "First the art set and now the Colorforms? We have to see how far this goes."

"Do we?" Ryan all but pleaded. "Do we really?"

"Of course we do," Ernest said.

13

LAWN MOWER MUSINGS

Eddie Wilmette's lawn was huge and took forever to mow. But today Ryan didn't care. It gave him lots of time to think, and lately there'd been a lot for Ryan to think about.

After Paige had told her story to the class a couple of weeks ago, more kids started going to the well. Not just kids from their class, either. Kids from other homerooms, other grades, other schools, even.

And all those kids had wishes. Over the last few weeks, Ryan, Ernest, and Lizzy had probably heard most of them. They had it down to a little routine. When the last bell rang, the three of them

133

met behind the school and then went into the woods, following the trails to the hidden cave.

Once inside the well, they'd listen to the wishes, sometimes for an hour or more. Afterward they'd leave, at which time Ernest would unfailingly forget his windbreaker and have to scurry back into the well to get it before they could walk to Ryan's house.

Ryan still didn't feel right about listening to the wishes, but Ernest was so certain it was the thing to do. And insistent. For a small, bony kid who weighed less than the average golden retriever, Ernest had a strange knack for asserting his will.

Many of the wishes were just ridiculous, outrageous requests for a Maserati or a million dollars. One kid wished for a pet lion. Aaron Robinette came back to wish for Bigfoot a couple more times.

But some of the wishes were really serious. One boy was worried about his older sister. She was in high school and hanging out with some other kids who smoked and ditched school, and maybe worse. The boy's sister and their parents were always yelling at each other, and he was afraid something bad was going to happen.

Another kid, a girl a grade ahead of them, came to Thompkins Well to make a wish for her cousin, a soldier who had served in Afghanistan for a year and a half. He'd been home about a month now and he was having trouble readjusting. He was moody and hard to talk to. He went jogging a lot and couldn't sleep at night.

It surprised Ryan how often people made wishes for others and not themselves. Those were the ones he remembered. For him, the wish that stuck the most was still that boy on the first day with Lizzy, the one whose dad was out of work and the family had all those bills and was trying to save up to send his mom to see his dying grandmother. He hadn't even recognized the kid's voice, but Ryan felt like he knew him, understood him.

That was the problem, though. He kept *thinking* about this stuff. He was getting sucked in. Especially after the business with Paige Barnett's brother and those ridiculous Colorforms. He was starting to wonder if Ernest might really be onto something.

And that scared him. Not because Ryan was against people catching a break for a change. But he was of the life philosophy that the light at the end of the tunnel was usually an oncoming train. For Ryan the other shoe never just dropped. The universe usually threw it at you.

A SATURDAY OF ONE'S OWN

One thing Lizzy could say for sure about this business with the well, it had certainly changed her Saturdays for the better. She had been hanging out with Ryan and Ernest almost daily for the last three weeks, so much so that she had been able to convince her mom to let her stay home alone this Saturday, provided Mrs. Hardy was going to be around in case of an emergency.

Today was the first Saturday in months that Lizzy didn't have to deal with her aunt and her cousin, and she was in heaven. She had the whole house to herself, even though all she did was eat cereal, read, and stay in her pajamas until eleven thirty.

That was when Mrs. Hardy called and invited her over to lunch. She and Mrs. Wilmette were sitting in the kitchen drinking coffee when Lizzy arrived. Lizzy played with Declan while the moms made lunch. Ryan was across the street mowing the Wilmette lawn while Ernest was up in his grandfather's attic. This was the usual routine; the three of them would go into the well during the week, and then Ernest would search the attic for "inspiration."

Ryan always snorted when Ernest said that, but Ernest didn't seem to let it bother him. Lizzy couldn't get over how persistently hopeful that kid was. She also couldn't get over how infectious his hopefulness could be.

Not that Lizzy was completely sold on the whole idea. She was still a very rational person at heart and not one to believe in fairy tales. Still, something strange was going on in Cliffs Donnelly.

Things around town were getting better, or at least feeling better. People seemed happier, upbeat. The difference wasn't huge, but it was noticeable. Cliffs Donnelly was changing. Even her own mom had seemed less tired and run-down these last few weeks.

Then again, a Saturday away from Chelsea and Aunt Patty was enough to make anybody see the world differently.

TOO BIG FOR A BACKPACK

Ernest was getting nowhere. This was the second, no, third Saturday he'd come up to the attic, and it was looking to be the third Saturday he would come down empty-handed. With each passing weekend, he felt his confidence waning and his indecision growing, like it was all slipping away from him.

The smell of freshly cut grass wafted through the attic window from the backyard. It bothered Ernest that his parents never considered that he could take care of the lawn. Of course, his head did barely crest the handlebar on the lawn mower. And the size of the machine did intimidate him a tiny bit. But he wasn't ever going to grow at all if everyone kept treating him like a little kid. Ernest firmly believed that condescension could keep a kid small, and not just figuratively. That it could literally, physically stunt your growth.

But that was a worry for another day. Ernest was afraid that if he didn't come down with something soon, Ryan and Lizzy were going to stop helping him. Should he just grab something? Anything? It couldn't hurt. So far the only consistent part of what he'd been doing was that nothing went according to plan.

At least, nothing went according to *his* plan.

Once he took something out of the attic, the art set or the Colorforms, it somehow managed to wind up where it belonged. Which meant, in theory, that if he just took all the toys out of the attic, then things would eventually sort themselves out like they were meant to.

It wasn't a theory he was particularly keen to test, though.

Ernest took a breath and went back to the beginning. A magical beam of light had guided him to the art set, but there had been no light when he took the Colorforms. For that he'd used logic, assuming that if there was an order to which items he should take, it would probably be the order in which they were all stacked on the chair.

But here was the problem. The fire extinguisher and the ray gun were both resting, side by side, against the back of the chair. So which one would be next? The fire extinguisher was on the left, and we read left to right, so that would make the fire extinguisher next in line. But the box for the ray gun was lying on its side, which made it stick out a little farther, so it was technically closer. The fire extinguisher, meanwhile, didn't even feel like it was part of the pile. But at the same time, Ernest wanted to pick the ray gun, because it was pretty cool, so that might be clouding his judgment.

He remembered something his dad had said once about making tough decisions. "When in doubt, the harder choice is usually the right one."

Well, Ernest knew which one would be harder to carry.

Ryan would think it was stupid.

"A fire extinguisher?" Ryan said as they walked into his house. "That's stupid."

"Ryan!" Lizzy scolded. She'd come to get them for lunch.

Ryan rolled his eyes. "Where is it?"

"I left it on the back porch," Ernest said. "It's kind of heavy."

"So, what? Now you just bring it to school and see what happens?"

Ernest sulked. "When you say it like that, it doesn't really sound like much of a plan, huh?"

Back at Ryan's they sat down to turkey sandwiches and corn chips. Mrs. Wilmette left to run some errands while Mrs. Hardy put Declan down for a nap.

Ryan had a little of Grandpa Eddie's lawn left to mow, so after they ate, the three of them went back over there. Ryan finished up, and then Ernest showed them the fire extinguisher.

"Wow," Lizzy said. "It's an antique."

Ryan said, "It's big."

It *was* big. Almost three feet tall and a good six inches in diameter at the base of the cylinder.

"They had to be back then," Lizzy explained. "The compression system alone—"

"I mean it's *too* big," Ryan said.

"He's right," Ernest said. "I'll never get that into school."

"Can't exactly hide it under your bed, either," Ryan said.

"I know," Lizzy said after some thought. "We can keep it in the well. No one will find it there, right? At least until we figure out what to do with it."

TOOLS (THE OTHER KIND)

Ernest, Ryan, and Lizzy took turns carrying the old copper fire extinguisher as they walked into the woods behind the school.

It was Ernest's shift when they stumbled upon the high school kids. There were four of them, two guys and two girls. They were smoking cigarettes and drinking, of all things, peppermint schnapps. Ryan tried not to dwell on the irony.

"Come on," he said. "We should get out of here."

They picked up the pace, but one of the guys spotted them. "Hey, come back here, you little punks!"

The two guys were typical burnout idiots. Ryan knew, though, that sometimes tools like this could be more trouble than the real tough kids. It's always the posers who take things too far.

Ryan really hated running from them. But he had Lizzy and Ernest to think about. It was the smart thing to do.

The burnouts started to give chase while the two girls tried to call them back. The idiots made a show of it, running hard like they really cared about catching a bunch of sixth graders. A few seconds later they were slowing down and hacking so hard Ryan thought they'd cough up a lung.

"We see you again, we're gonna kick your little butts!" one of them called out.

"Tools," Ryan muttered as he, Lizzy, and Ernest caught their breath. He looked around. They'd run onto a different trail, one that looped back toward the school. Doubling back would risk crossing the burnouts again.

Ryan didn't have much trouble convincing Ernest and Lizzy to forgo the well for the day. That's when Ernest realized that he didn't have the fire extinguisher anymore.

"I'm sorry," he said, hanging his head in shame. "I dropped it when we started running."

"Don't be sorry," Ryan said. "It was smart. We can't go look for it, though. Not today, at least."

They continued on the trail until it led them back out of the woods a couple of hundred yards from where they'd entered.

By the time they returned to Ryan's, Mrs. Wilmette was back

from her errands. A little while later Lizzy's mom came over, still in her hospital scrubs, and the three moms sat in the kitchen talking for the rest of the afternoon. Ryan didn't know what they were talking about, but they clearly didn't want to be bothered. Any time he came into the kitchen to get something from the fridge, his mom shooed him out of the room.

Ryan, Lizzy, and Ernest watched TV and drank soda in the den for a while. But Ernest was still down about losing the fire extinguisher.

Luckily, Ryan had an idea that would cheer him up.

14

ROLLO STORIES

"More lemonade, anyone?" Mrs. Haemmerle said, holding the pitcher up for takers. Their mouths full of cookies, Ernest, Ryan, and Lizzy all held out their glasses for a refill.

Ernest had been down about losing the fire extinguisher in the woods, but he forgot all about that as soon as Ryan came in from the kitchen, turned off the TV, and announced that they were all going over to Mrs. Haemmerle's house. Ever since Ernest had first met the old woman, he'd wanted to go back to her house and talk to her some more.

The kids had been gorging on cookies and lemonade for the last half hour while Ernest asked questions about Rollo.

Mrs. Haemmerle explained that because of Rollo's enlarged heart, he was never expected to live long enough to become an adult. The grown-ups all seemed to know this, but none of the kids did.

Some things never change, Ernest thought.

A couple of days later, Ryan told Ernest that Mrs. Haemmerle wanted them to come over again next Saturday.

"Okay," Ernest said. "Did she say why?"

Ryan shook his head. "Just said to bring you over."

"She say anything else?"

Ryan shook his head again. Actually, Mrs. Haemmerle had told him to bring "his little girlfriend" along as well. He kept that part to himself.

This time when the kids came over to Mrs. Haemmerle's house, she wasn't alone. There was an old man with her, probably as old as Mrs. Haemmerle, more or less.

"Kids, this is Jack Hought," Mrs. Haemmerle said.

Mr. Hought shook all their hands. "Nice to meet you all," he said. When he got to Ernest, he stopped and stared. "You weren't kidding, Annie," he said to Mrs. Haemmerle without taking his eyes off Ernest. "He looks so much like Rollo."

"Ernest, Jack here was Rollo's best friend. If you really want to hear stories about Rollo, he's your man."

BUDDY THE IDIOT

Buddy was an idiot. And Heather knew he was an idiot. It was kind of hard to miss. The guy liked to do three things: smoke cigarettes, break things, and wear this ugly brown parka with grimy fake fur along the hood, sleeves, and waistline.

At the present moment he was accomplishing all three at once. They were in the woods behind the middle school with Drake and Margo, like they were most afternoons. Sitting around and smoking. Truth be told, it was kind of boring.

Then Buddy found an old liquor bottle in the brush and started throwing it around. He threw it against the ground. Then he threw it against a tree. And then against a bigger tree. But it wouldn't break.

This bottle is getting the better of him, Heather thought.

Heather knew she couldn't keep doing this. Over the last several weeks she'd been getting in trouble, kind of a lot. Skipping school, blowing off homework, fighting with her parents, breaking curfew. Two weeks ago, Drake got caught trying to steal beer from the grocery store. Heather didn't know he was doing it, but she was with him—they all were—so they all got busted.

Then last weekend, there was that business with those middle school kids. Buddy and Drake heard them walking on one of the nearby trails and chased them off. The kids ran, of course, but then Buddy, all worked up, kept yelling at them, like he was really mad or something. Heather didn't understand what he had to be so mad about.

Like why was he getting so mad about this dumb bottle?

"Heather, come over here," Buddy yelled to her. She went and found him standing over a large stone embedded in the ground. "Watch this. Here it comes."

He started winding up.

"No, Buddy, don't—"

But he was already yelling, "Boom!" and hurling the bottle down onto the stone. Heather reeled back, her hands shielding her face as the bottle shattered, sending shards of glass upward.

Heather got clear, but Buddy took a couple of shards in his cheek. He screeched, kind of girlishly, Heather couldn't help noticing, and dropped his cigarette onto a pile of dry leaves. Or, they had been dry leaves two minutes ago, before the half-empty bottle Buddy was throwing around drenched them with highly flammable alcohol.

The next thing they all knew, the leaves had caught on fire, filling the nearby woods with thick smoke.

Heather knew she should go to the fire, try to put it out, but she was disoriented by all the smoke. Margo and Drake grabbed her, and together they ran through the woods as fast as they could.

THE RUNNING MARINE

When Chad Finnegan was in the Marines, it seemed like all his unit ever did was run. They ran before breakfast, they ran after dinner, they ran when Sergeant Delaney wanted to keep them out of trouble. At the time, Chad had promised himself that once he was done with the Marines, he'd never run again.

But ever since he got back home, he'd been running every day. Sometimes twice a day. Mostly he liked to run in the woods out behind his old middle school.

Chad had been home for a month and a half, after serving in Afghanistan for eighteen. He'd enlisted in the Marines right out of high school, three years ago, with his best friend, Matt Redigger. They'd gone through basic training together and, after that, through jump school.

Then they'd gone to Afghanistan together, but only Chad had come back. Matt had been killed when his jeep ran over an IED, an improvised explosive device.

Now Chad was home, safe, but it didn't feel like home anymore. Oh, family and friends welcomed him back and shook his hand. Two old guys had even picked up his lunch tab last week. It was kind and he appreciated it. Still, he kept to himself when he could.

Running the trails helped. It cleared his mind, and it wore him out. Being tired helped the most.

He'd already run once this morning, but by noon he was getting restless again, so he decided to take another run through the woods before dinner. About halfway down the path, Chad heard some high school kids nearby. Then he heard a girl scream, and a lot of yelling. He stopped and saw tufts of smoke peeking up through the trees.

Chad ran back toward the screaming and the smoke. As he was closing in, he tripped over something on the path that rolled under his foot and threw his leg behind him and out of control. He went down hard but was back up again in a heartbeat.

He turned to see what he'd tripped over. It was a fire extinguisher, a really old one. It looked brand-new, though.

Chad picked it up and rushed toward the smoke.

MR. HOUGHT

Mr. Hought said, "It was on his ninth birthday."

They'd been sitting and talking for almost an hour, Mr. Hought telling story after story about him and Rollo and Mrs. Haemmerle. Sometimes Grandpa Eddie was in them, too. Many of the stories were funny, but even when the memories made Mr. Hought smile, there was a sadness behind it.

Perhaps because he knew that, eventually, he'd have to get to this part.

How Rollo died.

"There was going to be a big party at his house," Mr. Hought said. "But just before lunch, Rollo told his parents he was going to go take a nap, so he'd be rested up for all his friends. Rollo went up to his bedroom, and while he was asleep, his heart gave out. Meanwhile, people started showing up for the party. Rollo's mom went upstairs to get him . . ." Mr. Hought stopped. Then he said, quietly, "Sad day."

Lizzy's eyes filled with tears and even Ryan was getting choked up. Ernest, strangely, seemed too riveted by the story to get upset.

Mr. Hought thought for a moment and chuckled, but in a hollow, rueful way. "Yep, sad day."

Mrs. Haemmerle gasped a little. "Oh, Jack," she said, reaching out to him. "I'm so sorry. I completely forgot—"

"Now, now," he said, taking her hand and patting it reassuringly. "That's okay." Mr. Hought and Mrs. Haemmerle were quiet for a moment, and then Mr. Hought looked at the kids. "I should probably explain. You see, the day Rollo died was also the day my father left me and my mother."

"Why would he do that?" Ryan exclaimed, the words jumping out of his mouth.

Mr. Hought looked at Ryan curiously for a minute, but then he just shrugged. "I don't know, son," he said.

"Excuse me, sir," Ernest said, an odd expression on his face. "If you don't mind me asking, what did you get Rollo for his birthday?"

Mr. Hought did a double take. This was clearly not a question he expected the boy would ask. But it triggered something in the old man's mind and he was suddenly very invested in remembering the answer.

"Rollo had asked for a stuffed animal." His eyes got big as if the flood of memories were overloading his brain. "I remember," he continued. "When I came back home, after Rollo had been found in his room, I heard my parents arguing. My father was angry that we gave it away. Which doesn't make sense, because my mom had bought it for Rollo weeks before the party. But that night he packed a bag and left. And I never saw him again."

Mr. Hought got quiet, lost in deep thought.

"Sock monkey," he said, smacking his knee with satisfaction. "That's what it was. I got him a sock monkey."

SQUATCH!

Aaron Robinette had been walking the trails of the Nature Preserve for over an hour so far. He was just about to call it a day when he heard a girl screaming. Camera at the ready, Aaron ran down the trail toward the screams.

And then he saw it.

Through a cloud of smoke, a figure burst from the woods, flailing wildly against the trees and brush in its way. It was the size of a man, more or less, tall but gangly. Brown mostly, and covered in dirt and leaves. Tufts of fur poked out around its head, waist, and wrists, and it ran with a jerky, loping gait.

The urge to run away was overwhelming. But Aaron stood his ground resolutely, and recorded the creature as it passed by a mere twenty feet from where he stood.

It didn't notice him as it stumbled by, but it did make some pretty curious noises. Higher pitched than Aaron would have expected from a beast of that size.

ROLLO'S PRESENTS

"They're Rollo's presents?" Lizzy said. "The art set, the Colorforms . . . They were meant for him?"

Ryan glanced over at Ernest, who had a glazed look in his eyes. The kid had barely spoken a word since they had left Mrs. Haemmerle and Jack Hought and walked back to Ryan's house.

Lizzy's mom had come over, and now she and Ryan's mom and Mrs. Wilmette sat in the kitchen having coffee and talking. They couldn't have cared less what the kids were doing, but Ryan still kept darting his head toward the doorway to make sure they didn't come out and overhear anything.

"But that would mean," Lizzy continued, turning her attention directly to Ernest, "that your grandfather kept all the old presents from Rollo's last birthday tucked away in his attic for sixty years? Why?"

Ernest, still lost in thought, didn't answer her.

"Well, someone say something," Lizzy snapped.

"You're asking the wrong questions," Ryan said.

Lizzy scowled. "Then what's the right question, Sherlock?" she asked huffily.

"Is there a sock monkey in Eddie's attic?"

KINDRED SPIRITS

By the time Fire Chief Nate Collins arrived on the scene, the fire in the Cliffs Donnelly Nature Preserve had been contained and extinguished. To call this good news would be a serious understatement. A fire in these woods could easily have spread out of control, particularly during this time of year, when the ground was dry and full of dead leaves and brush.

The source of this good fortune was a passerby, a jogger who had put out the fire single-handedly with a fire extinguisher he'd found in the woods.

A vintage Elkhart Brass copper fire extinguisher.

It looked to be mid-century, and even had the brass nameplate on the front with the blue writing. The fire chief couldn't believe the thing had actually worked.

Nate's team confirmed the fire had been started by a cigarette dropped into a pile of leaves. Some rum from a bottle broken nearby had acted as an accelerant.

Luckily, someone had been around to do something about it. Nate personally thanked the young man who'd stopped the fire. He could tell from his posture and the way he carried himself that the jogger, a serious, respectful young man named Chad, was a soldier. Nate guessed Marines and was right.

He guessed something else and was right about that as well—that the kid had seen combat, and that it had followed him back home. Nate, too, had been a Marine. He'd done two tours in the First Gulf War. He remembered how hard it had been to return to civilian life, especially in the beginning.

Nate drove Chad home himself. As the young Marine got out of the car, Nate asked him if he had ever given any thought to becoming a firefighter.

Chad was caught off guard by the question. "Not since I was a kid, sir," he said, smiling just a little.

HEATHER AND HER BRAIN HAVE A LITTLE TALK

Stupid. Stupid. Stupid. What was she even doing smoking in the woods, hanging out with guys who liked to break things and scare little kids? And what was she doing with "friends" who thought all that stuff was fun?

Heather thought she knew what it felt like to want something. To really, really want something. But until today Heather had never wanted anything so badly, so desperately, as she just wanted everything to be all right again. To make this stupid afternoon disappear.

Later that evening, when she learned that the fire had been put out and no one had been hurt, she felt overwhelming relief.

It's time to stop being stupid, her brain told her. And this time, Heather listened.

PROOF!

The footage would be a bit shaky, so once Aaron uploaded it to his computer, he'd need to go through it frame by frame, scrutinizing every detail. The smoke and the trees had both obscured his view, but Aaron was nonetheless confident that he'd just recorded the single most important piece of Bigfoot evidence since the Patterson-Gimlin film of 1967.

By the time he finally made his way out of the trails on the edge of North Side Park, the fire trucks were already pulling into the little parking lot by the jungle gyms.

Two of the firefighters were keen to ask Aaron questions, starting with what he was doing in the park. There probably would have been more questions to follow, but after Aaron said he had been searching for Bigfoot, the men just looked at each other and told him to go on home.

THE MONKEY

Because it's what adults always do, just as Ernest, Ryan, and Lizzy had been about to slip over to Grandpa Eddie's to get the sock monkey, the mothers decided it was time to break up their little coffee klatch and go home.

It looked like the sock monkey and Mr. Hought would have to wait for another day.

But then the kids' luck was changed by, of all things, the sirens from at least three fire trucks barreling down the street a few blocks away. The sirens woke Declan from his afternoon nap, and soon Declan was in the kitchen being fussed over by the three mothers, leaving Ryan and his friends, once again, conveniently forgotten.

Well, almost.

"Ryan, honey," his mother called to him just as he, Ernest, and Lizzy were about to make a break for it. "Your father and Mr. Wilmette are working late again, so we're going to do Chinese takeout here." She thrust a menu and a notepad into Ryan's hands. "Find out what your friends want, okay?"

It wasn't until after dinner that the kids finally had a window to sneak away to Grandpa Eddie's house.

Ryan and Lizzy waited downstairs while Ernest went into the attic. The sock monkey was sitting in the rocking chair, leaning against the quilt, both encased in tightly sealed plastic bags to protect them from moths and dust. Through the plastic, he could see a string with a card attached tied around the monkey's neck. On the card, written in a young boy's hurried scrawl, Ernest read:

To my best friend in the whole world.

   - Jack

Ernest breathed a sigh of relief. The way Rollo's gifts had a tendency to disappear on him, he hadn't taken for granted that the sock monkey would still be there.

Even better, he thought, this time I won't need to figure out which one to pick next.

15

A SCIENTIFIC DEBATE

"Dude, it wasn't Bigfoot."

"Shut up, Jamie," Aaron said. "You just can't admit that I got documented footage—"

"Documented footage?" Jamie cackled. "Right."

"It's blurry because of the smoke. And the trees. And because he's running really fast."

"And because it's a guy in a bear suit."

They'd been at it ever since first bell, and homeroom was no different. The other night Aaron had burned a DVD of some footage he shot in the woods that, he claimed, proved the existence of the infamous Sasquatch.

To say that Aaron and Jamie disagreed on this point would be putting it mildly.

"You just can't admit you're wrong." There was a slight crack in Aaron's voice. He was getting upset.

"You just can't admit you're nuts," Jamie said.

Ryan was just glad for a distraction, something to steer talk away from Thompkins Well, at least for a little while. Especially since the local news was now making a big deal out of the ex-Marine hero who put out the fire in the Cliffs Donnelly Nature Preserve with an antique fire extinguisher he found lying in the woods.

More than the art set or the Colorforms, the fire extinguisher got to Ryan. He'd held it in his own hands. He was right beside Ernest when Ernest dropped it in the woods. He knew firsthand *that* was real. It had happened. But at the same time, the more he knew, the less sense it all made. How did this connect with the well? What kind of wish could possibly involve a random fire in the woods?

On the other side of Mr. Earle's classroom, away from the increasingly heated Bigfoot debate, Winston and Tommy huddled intently over Winston's drawing pad. Those two were up to something, Ryan could tell, though which one was corrupting the other remained, at present, unclear.

Yesterday he'd seen them wandering around the school's courtyard with a tape measure in a very focused and determined manner.

With any luck, this would all be over once they gave the sock monkey to Mr. Hought. Ryan figured (or rather, desperately hoped) that the sock monkey would be the end of it. The stuffed animal had to be the reason Ernest's grandfather had sent him up to the attic, to find and give it back to his little brother's best friend. Maybe the other stuff, the art set and the Colorforms and the granted wishes, were just flukes, coincidences, and nothing more.

Ryan wasn't big on the idea of coincidences, but if the alternative was Ernest's "magic," he was willing to consider anything.

The plan was for Ryan, Ernest, and Lizzy to bring the sock monkey to Mrs. Haemmerle's on Friday and give it to Jack then. Lizzy's mom had already asked if Lizzy could come over Friday night while she went to a work function. Ryan figured they might as well make a party of it and invited Ernest to sleep over. Ernest got so excited he practically squealed. Man, he was a weird kid.

Then again, if they could be done with this whole Thompkins Well business by Friday, Ryan just might squeal with excitement himself.

SOCK MONKEY SURPRISE

On Friday afternoon the kids brought the sock monkey to Mrs. Haemmerle. But when she called Mr. Hought's house, she got no answer. Then she remembered. "That's right," she said, lightly smacking her forehead. "It's Friday."

"What's Friday?" Lizzy asked.

"Jack visits Shady Lanes every Friday. It's an assisted living facility."

The kids deflated, especially Ernest. He'd misplaced all the other items he'd brought down from the attic, and he wanted to get this one to the old man before he found a way to screw it up like he had with the art set. And the Colorforms. And the fire extinguisher.

"Well," Mrs. Haemmerle said, grabbing her keys off the kitchen counter. "Let's go."

About twenty minutes later they pulled into Shady Lanes and found Mr. Hought sitting out on a veranda with a very old man in a wheelchair. Mr. Hought and Mrs. Haemmerle were old, but this guy was another level of old. He was, like, Bible old. Mr. Hought was taking great care with the man, fixing the blanket on his legs, pouring him iced tea, wheeling his chair out of the sun. When Mr. Hought saw Mrs. Haemmerle and the kids, he stood up, surprised but not displeased to see them.

"Jack," Mrs. Haemmerle began. "Ernest here found something he thought you might like to see."

Ernest gave Mr. Hought the sock monkey. Mr. Hought's eyes grew huge and his hands trembled as he took the sock monkey from the boy.

"My God," Mr. Hought said. "Where . . . How . . . ?"

"My grandfather's attic," Ernest said. "It's been sitting up there all this time."

Mr. Hought took the sock monkey out of the plastic. His eyes teared while his hands worried the stuffed animal, as if the more he touched it, the more he remembered about the last time he'd seen it.

Mr. Hought returned his attention to the old man in the wheelchair. "Stanley, you remember Annie."

"Hello there, Stanley." Mrs. Haemmerle kissed him on his cheek.

"And this is Ernest, Ryan, and Lizzy. Ernest is Eddie Wilmette's grandson."

The old man smiled warmly. "Nice to meet you all."

"Kids," Mr. Hought said. "This is Detective Stanley Donan."

Detective Donan chuckled. "Retired."

Mr. Hought kept squeezing the sock monkey as he talked. "Stanley here, he . . . Well, after my father left, he looked after me and my mom."

"Were you friends with Mr. Hought's dad?" Lizzy asked.

Detective Donan considered how best to answer. "Well, I can't say we were friends, exactly. But you could say there was a mutual regard."

"I should explain," Mr. Hought interjected. "My father was a criminal."

"Well, yes," Detective Donan said. "Technically. Ben Mattingly was what we used to call a second-story man. A cat burglar. A very good cat burglar."

"And you arrested him?" Ernest guessed.

Detective Donan chuckled. "Oh, no. Ben was too good for a small-town beat cop like me to ever catch. Lucky for me he never pooped where he ate, if you know what I mean."

Ryan and Ernest didn't.

"He means that Ben Mattingly never pulled any jobs in Cliffs Donnelly," Lizzy explained.

Detective Donan gave her an impressed nod. "Worked out of Chicago mostly. Indianapolis, too." The old detective was enjoying talking shop again. "He was very cautious."

"That was why he had a different last name?" Lizzy guessed.

"Bingo," Detective Donan said. "In case anyone came looking for him."

Mr. Hought, meanwhile, was poking a spot on the sock monkey, back near the tail.

"Something wrong?" Mrs. Haemmerle asked.

"Some of the stuffing must have hardened. Feels like there's a rock in here."

"Give it over," Detective Donan said, motioning for the stuffed animal. He took his glasses out of his shirt pocket and examined the sock monkey, paying particular attention to the stitching.

"Young man—Ryan, is it?"

"Yes, sir."

"There's a lady sitting about thirty feet behind me, knitting a sweater for her granddaughter."

"I see her," Ryan said.

"Tell her that Stanley would like to borrow her seam ripper."

Ryan did as he was told. The grandmother gave him the seam ripper and he delivered it to Detective Donan.

"What is it?" Mr. Hought asked.

"This stitching here." Detective Donan pointed. "It's not the original."

He laid the sock monkey on his lap. Very delicately, he eased apart the stitching, reached inside, and pulled out a large red gem about the diameter of a silver dollar.

"Well, I'll be double dipped," the old man said, amazed.

Mr. Hought's knees buckled. "Is that the Holyoke Red Diamond?"

Detective Donan held it up to the light. "I believe it is."

Mrs. Haemmerle and the kids were completely shocked. Mr. Hought and Detective Donan were both surprised and, in a way, not surprised at all.

"They must have been close," Detective Donan said.

"He really . . . He did it for us," Mr. Hought said, his voice barely above a whisper.

"Oh, for Pete's sake, boys!" Mrs. Haemmerle exclaimed. "Share it with the class, will you?"

THE HOLYOKE RED DIAMOND

"'The Holyoke Red Diamond was stolen in 1952 from the private vault of Chicago dry goods magnate Eustace Holyoke,'" Lizzy read from Ernest's cell phone. They were all back in Detective Donan's room now. "'At the time of its disappearance it was valued at fourteen million dollars'!"

Mrs. Haemmerle, speaking for most of them, yelped.

Lizzy scanned ahead to the end of the article. "It goes on to say that the Holyoke Red Diamond was never recovered." She looked up at the group. "So for roughly the last six decades, one of the rarest jewels in the world has been hidden inside a sock monkey?"

Mr. Hought chuckled. "In Eddie Wilmette's attic. How's that

for a kick in the head?" Then his face clouded. "So, it was Muldoon," Mr. Hought said in a low voice.

Detective Donan nodded gravely.

"Who the heck's Muldoon?!" Ryan hadn't meant to blurt it out like that, but he could tell by the way the old men were looking at each other that the Holyoke Red Diamond was only half the story.

"I couldn't prove it, of course, but the minute I heard about the heist, I knew it was Ben." The old detective looked at the Holyoke Red Diamond as if he was looking into the past. "The only fence this side of New York City who could move a rock that hot," he continued, "was a guy out of Chicago named Orson Muldoon."

Ryan leaned his head toward Lizzy. "A fence is someone who buys and sells stolen goods," she said, anticipating the question.

"Thanks," Ryan murmured.

"Though we could never prove it," Mr. Hought said, "we've always suspected that Muldoon double-crossed my dad and killed him to get the diamond."

Detective Donan said, "The day before Ben skipped town, a car with Illinois plates was pulled over for speeding on State Route 72 just outside Cliffs Donnelly. Inside were two men."

"Muldoon's men," Lizzy guessed.

Detective Donan nodded. "They didn't have any outstanding

warrants, and they were too smart to travel with any weapons in the car. The officer who pulled them over knew the two men were hitters, and that they were looking for Ben. But he didn't have cause to arrest them."

"So he let them go?"

"He had to."

"Wait a minute," Ryan said. "You were the officer, weren't you?"

Detective Donan had the look of a man who wishes he could have done things differently but deep down knows it still wouldn't have changed anything.

"And when you couldn't arrest the hit men," Lizzy filled in the blanks, "you did the next best thing. You warned Ben Mattingly."

"I did." Detective Donan shook his head. "I'm guessing Ben's plan was to take his family and disappear with the diamond."

Lizzy, working ahead, gasped. "But by then Mr. Hought had already given the sock monkey, and with it the Holyoke Red Diamond, to Rollo Wilmette."

"Wait, you're saying this poor guy died because he hid the diamond in the wrong stuffed animal?" Ryan said.

"That," Detective Donan said slowly, "would not be inaccurate."

"Taking the time to get the sock monkey back from the

Wilmette house would have been too risky," Lizzy reasoned gently. "It could have put both the Wilmettes and his own family in danger."

"So he went back to Chicago," Ryan filled in. "To lure the hit men away from his family."

"His body was fished out of the Chicago River three days after he skipped town. Bullet to the back of the head."

Ernest, who had been silent all this time, finally spoke. "He sacrificed himself to protect his family," he said quietly.

"And yours, too, my boy," Detective Donan added. "After a fashion."

"Whatever happened to Muldoon?" Lizzy said.

"Funny, that," Detective Donan said. "A few months later he turned up dead as well. Rumor has it he tried to fence a copy of the Holyoke Red Diamond and made some dangerous people pretty angry."

"Ben Mattingly gave him a fake before he was killed?" Ryan said.

"It stands to reason," Detective Donan said. "Let Muldoon think he's won. That way he stops looking for it and has no reason to come back to Cliffs Donnelly."

Ryan looked over at Mr. Hought, who had retreated from the conversation. To his surprise, the man was smiling.

"And here I thought I'd wasted a quarter all those years ago," he said, giving Mrs. Haemmerle a little wink.

"Thompkins Well," Mrs. Haemmerle said softly, remembering.

"What?" Lizzy and Ryan responded in unison.

"In our day people used to throw coins in the old Thompkins Well and make wishes," Mrs. Haemmerle explained to the kids.

"You don't say," Ryan said dryly.

"If you don't mind my asking, Mr. Hought," Lizzy said, "what exactly did you wish for?"

"Like he said the other day," Mr. Hought said, cocking his head in Ryan's direction, "I just wanted to know why."

A PRACTICAL PLAN

Eventually, the conversation returned to the elephant in the room, namely, a stolen gem that, according to Lizzy's research, was worth more money than a small-market professional football team.

The group quickly agreed that Mr. Hought and Detective Donan would turn the Holyoke Red Diamond over to the proper authorities. Ernest, Lizzy, and Ryan's involvement in finding the gem would remain a secret among the six of them.

"Best to say that Jack here found it among some old things," Detective Donan reasoned. He looked at Ernest. "No one needs to know it was in your grandad's house all this time. Your dad's got a lot on his plate, and he doesn't need a distraction like this right now."

Ernest wasn't sure how to take that. It bothered him that the adults were making this decision *for* him and not *with* him, especially since he was the one who had found the sock monkey in the first place and hand delivered it, along with the Holyoke Red Diamond, right to them.

What bothered Ernest even more was that he didn't understand why Detective Donan said what he did about Ernest's dad.

But what bothered him most of all was that Ryan and Lizzy seemed to know exactly what the old detective was talking about.

AARON ROBINETTE IS UNDETERRED

Aaron Robinette hated Jamie Dahl. He was Aaron's best friend, but Aaron still hated him. Hated the way he'd humiliated Aaron in front of the whole class, mocked his footage, made them all laugh. The jerk.

When Aaron got agitated or self-conscious, his body would get restless. If he was sitting, his legs would start bouncing so fast the floor beneath him would vibrate. His arms would tighten and he'd press his palms up against his forehead as hard as he could, leaving red splotches over his eyes.

Right now he was very agitated. Every muscle in his arms, legs, and neck squeezed as he felt the kind of overpowering frustration that can only be tamed by breaking something large and important. He looked over at his desk and nearly grabbed his computer and threw it on the floor.

But he didn't. That computer was insanely expensive. His parents had bought it for him last Christmas in the hopes that shamelessly throwing technology at him might direct his dogged imagination away from monster hunting and a possible college degree in medieval folklore and toward, well, just about anything else.

It was a beautiful piece of machinery, with an operating system that had enough power to do all kinds of things. Like position a satellite or manage the traffic systems for a major metropolitan area or . . .

Run the latest in image-enhancing software.

THE PRETTY MUCH

"Your dad's trying to get a loan from the bank to save the factory," said Ryan. "That's what your dad and my dad have been working on the last few weeks. Why they haven't been around."

They were standing outside the retirement home waiting for Mrs. Haemmerle to finish talking to the men. Ernest was feeling that particular brand of irritation where a little bit of knowledge makes you feel dumber than you did when you had no idea what was going on at all.

"Your dad told you that?" Ernest said.

"Ernest, the whole town pretty much knows all about it."

Ernest felt his cheeks flush, as what had been merely embarrassing a moment ago was now humiliating on a positively thermonuclear scale. The whole town?

The whole town, of course, except for him.

He must be the *pretty much*.

"So you can see how a news story about a priceless, stolen red diamond in your late grandfather's attic would look bad," Lizzy said, putting a comforting arm around Ernest's shoulder. "People wouldn't understand why your dad needs the loan if you have rare jewels and who knows what else hidden in your house."

Ernest started to protest, but then Mrs. Haemmerle came out of the retirement home. The adults had decided the simplest thing to do would be to stick to the actual story up to the point where Ben Mattingly hid the Holyoke Red Diamond in the sock monkey. But Mr. Hought would leave out the part about giving the sock monkey to Rollo as a birthday present. Instead, he would say that it had been his all along, and that he had recently discovered it buried in an overlooked box of mementos from his late mother's house. Like the best lies, it was close to the truth. Which meant it was easier to remember, and more likely to withstand scrutiny.

Ernest sulked the entire ride back from Shady Lanes. Realizing that he was *pretty much* the only person in town not to know about the precarious state of his own family's business put him in a bit of a funk.

But then, once they got back to Ryan's house, Ernest saw his mother there with his overnight bag and the pot of chili Mrs. Hardy had going on the stove, and remembered about the sleepover. And suddenly his spirits lifted.

His first sleepover!

As the kids said goodbye to Mrs. Hardy and Mrs. Wilmette, who were going over to Lizzy's house to help her mom get ready for a work event, Ernest realized something. It had been a great day, a magical day. What else could you call it? A diamond hidden inside a sock monkey, an amazing story with thieves and killers and a father who gave up his own life to save his family—this day had *everything*.

Of course the bit about keeping what they did a secret was a downer, but even that was all right because he had friends. Friends who were perfectly content to eat chili and watch action movies with him all evening, and pretended not to notice when he looked away at the scary parts. Friends who didn't treat him like a baby, friends who had believed in him, and friends, he was now convinced, who were going to stay his friends even though his business with the well was over.

And it *was* over. Ernest felt that more powerfully than any feeling he'd had since this all started. As he drifted off to sleep, curled up in a beanbag chair in front of the T.V, he *knew* he'd never go back inside Thompkins Well again. The way it went down today with the sock monkey, the symmetry and closure and the we-will-never-speak-of-this-again conversation they'd had with Mr. Hought and Detective Donan, everything convinced him that this was the big finale.

He'd fulfilled his grandfather's legacy.

THE FALSE CALM

Later that night, when everyone else was asleep and Ryan was watching one last movie in the recliner, he felt content, for the first time in a long while. That sock monkey, it seemed, had wrapped up the whole Thompkins Well business in a neat little bow.

From here, Ryan was sure, things would start getting back to normal. But a different normal. Maybe a normal that was just a little better than the one before.

The movie Ryan was watching—well, only half watching

because he was getting pretty sleepy himself—was a thriller about a detective who falls in love with a woman he's trying to protect from a serial killer terrorizing the city. Ryan had learned from his dad that a common device in these kinds of movies was a plot twist called the false calm, a trick ending whereby the killer is either caught or killed so that the hero will let his guard down, only to then discover that the police arrested the wrong guy or the killer faked his death and that everyone is now in even worse danger than before.

The movie Ryan was watching happened to employ just such a false calm, but he fell asleep before he got to that part.

16

TODAY'S TOP STORY!

By Monday, the jewel-pooping sock monkey was one of the top news stories in the country. And why not? It had a little bit of everything. It was incredible, it was funny, and it was heartwarming, but with a backstory of suspense, danger, and tragedy.

Not to mention that "jewel-pooping sock monkey" had a really catchy ring to it.

Shortly after the federal authorities announced the return of the diamond, the story was picked up nationally, and for a while there, Cliffs Donnelly was kind of big news. Jack Hought and Detective Stanley Donan (Ret.) received a modest reward from the Holyoke Foundation and even appeared on a couple of talk shows, during which Mr. Hought told the story of how he visited Thompkins Well as a boy to ask what had happened to his dad. It was quite the crowd-pleaser.

Ryan really wished the old man hadn't done that, but he couldn't blame the guy. And it didn't seem to have done any harm.

Besides, even if Mr. Hought hadn't said the well was responsible for finding the diamond, everyone else in Cliffs Donnelly would have assumed as much anyway. By now, across Cliffs Donnelly, from North Side to South, Thompkins Well was all anyone was talking about.

Like some kid in line at the movies:

"I went to Thompkins Well because my sister was hanging with these burnouts in the woods and getting in trouble and stuff. And, like, a week later she completely stopped hanging out with them and things are cool again."

Or a group of girls out in front of school:

"My cousin was a Marine and he was in the Nature Preserve during that fire. He put it out with a fire extinguisher he found on the ground and now he's with the fire department!"

Or Aaron Robinette:

"Just you wait, guys . . . It's Bigfoot. I'll show you all!"

Everyone was talking about the well these days. And not just kids anymore, either. The forgotten old landmark was now the talk of the town. Like a local sports team or an upcoming civic event, it was a conversation starter, something to gossip about in a coffee shop or a hair salon.

Everywhere he went, it seemed, Ryan couldn't escape the chatter. He even took to humming loudly in the hallways between classes just to keep from hearing any other kids talk about the wishes they made or were granted. Until, finally, when Ryan seriously considered faking an illness just to stay home and get some peace and quiet, it all seemed to stop. The story about a small-town wishing well and a priceless jewel hidden in a stuffed monkey's butt had run its course, and people turned their attention to other things.

And that was more than fine with Ryan. Even Ernest was surprisingly keen to take a step back. It was settled, then.

Ryan, Ernest, and Lizzy agreed they would not return to Thompkins Well.

SHIFT CHANGES

Tommy Bricks's parents started leaving him home alone when he was six. Some of this was logistical. His dad worked the line at a factory that made kitchen appliances and preferred second shift (four to midnight) so he could hit the bars afterward, sleep during the day, and then leave again before Tommy got home from school. His mom worked first shift but took a lot of overtime, so sometimes she didn't come home until Tommy had already gone to sleep.

In the end, only Sam had ever looked out for him, doing the best he could while trying to go to school and hold down a job at the same time. He taught Tommy how to work the stove and the oven, the washer and dryer.

How to take care of himself.

Living alone at the age of six is not a good thing for a kid. Tommy was lonely in a way that most people could never begin to grasp. He kept the TV on a lot, even when he wasn't watching it. The voices filled some of the empty space in the house.

Kids are resilient, a cold-comfort truth if ever there was one, and over time, Tommy adapted to his situation. He got good at being alone. So when Winston Patil first started coming home with him after school, it was an adjustment.

When they first brought their idea to Mr. Earle, Tommy was sure that the teacher would shoot it down. Not that he thought Mr. Earle was a bad guy or anything. He definitely treated Tommy better than any other teacher at the school. Tommy was just used to hearing no from adults.

Mr. Earle, however, not only loved the idea but offered to be their teacher-advisor on the project. For the first few days, they met with him after school. Tommy and Winston showed him sketches of what they wanted to do. Winston was very thorough.

By the end of the week, Mr. Earle told them he'd heard enough. "Get to work," he said. "I'm here if you need me."

Ever since, Winston had been walking home with Tommy. With the house to themselves, Tommy would work in the garage while Winston did more sketching at the kitchen table. Even though they sometimes went hours without seeing each other, Tommy still enjoyed having Winston around.

But then Tommy's dad got into an "altercation" with the day foreman and was moved to third shift (midnight to eight a.m.). According to the union rep, his dad would have to stay on the night shift for at least three months before he could apply for a transfer back to the swing shift.

What this all meant for Tommy was that his dad would now be home in the afternoons, probably until dinnertime, when he would then go out and drink until his shift started at midnight.

And that meant Tommy and Winston couldn't keep working at his house, not any longer.

GUESS WHO'S COMING TO SNACK TIME

A month ago, opening the front door to find Tommy Bricks and Winston Patil standing on his porch would have seemed beyond weird to Ryan.

Today, though, it barely registered above mild disbelief on Ryan's things-I-didn't-see-coming Richter scale.

"Uh, hey, guys," Ryan said. "Come on in."

Tommy motioned Winston ahead and then followed him inside.

"Thanks, Hardy," Tommy said. "I . . . kinda need a favor."

Back at the bottom of the porch steps, Ryan saw an old wagon filled with junk, as in actual discarded items one would find in a junkyard: pieces of metal, stones and bricks, rebar, broken home appliances, and a lot of automobile parts. Good, old-fashioned junk.

Tommy followed Ryan's eyes to the wagon. Then, with something between a growl and a clearing of the throat, he explained. He and Winston were doing a project for school (he didn't offer specifics) and they needed somewhere to work. Until recently they'd been at Tommy's house, where they had the place to themselves. But last week Tommy's dad got moved to third shift, meaning he now might be around when the boys came home from school.

"And, you know," Tommy said, nodding his head in Winston's direction.

Ryan knew. How Tommy's dad would react to seeing a kid like Winston in his house was anybody's guess, though *everybody's* guess would be some variation of very, very badly. In addition to being mean, violent, and alcoholic, Tommy's dad was also, like a lot of people in Cliffs Donnelly, a person who divided the world into stark categories of "us" and "them." And the "them" all looked more or less like Winston Patil.

"My house is no good, either," Winston chimed in. His grandmother had just come all the way from India to live with Winston's family, and her two preferred ways to settle into her new environment were cooking and telling Winston that whatever he was doing was too dangerous, too messy, or a dubious use of his time. Since Tommy pretty much personified each of those three categories all by himself, Winston's house wouldn't work.

"So," Tommy said, cocking his head toward the wagon. "You got anyplace we can unload all this stuff?"

Ryan led them around back to the garage. Strangely, it never occurred to him to say no. He did wonder, though, why Tommy had come to his house. Ryan figured it was probably a combination of three things: (1) Tommy felt like Ryan owed him one for not beating him up that day after school, (2) he felt a unique connection to Ryan as someone he had once considered beating up but didn't, and (3) there wasn't anyplace else to go within walking distance.

"Cool. Thanks, Hardy," Tommy said in a way that suggested Ryan wouldn't be sticking around.

Ryan left them to it and went back inside through the kitchen, where his mom was filling a juice cup for Declan.

"Ryan," his mom said, a bit perplexed as she peered out the kitchen window at the two boys meticulously assembling pieces of trash in the middle of the garage. "Do you have friends over?"

"Sort of," Ryan said, plopping down at the table. As his mind worked over how to explain things to his mom, he found himself stuck on an unwelcome thought. Tommy had banked on Ryan understanding his predicament concerning Winston. Was it because Tommy assumed that Ryan's dad was a lot like Mr. Bricks? Statistically speaking, for their neighborhood, it was probably an even bet on Tommy's part. Would his own dad have a problem with Winston being over at their house?

It was a thought Ryan never would have had a year ago.

"Is the big one Tommy Bricks?" his mother asked, still staring out the window in curious confusion.

Ryan explained the general situation—school project, Winston's overbearing grandmother, and Tommy's father (which needed no further explanation beyond the words *shift change*).

"Okay," his mom said, turning her attention back to Ryan. "Grab the bread from the pantry and help me put some sandwiches together."

"I think they just want to be left alone, Mom," Ryan tried to explain.

"I don't care. They're still our guests," she said, taking the bread from him and going to work on some PB&Js. A few minutes later she opened the back door and called out to Winston and Tommy. "Boys! Come in for a snack."

"Mom . . ." Ryan groaned.

Though one had been raised by carrot and the other by stick, Winston and Tommy had both learned well to come directly when a mother calls. Winston promptly introduced himself to Ryan's mom, which earned Ryan a disapproving look for not being quicker on the draw, manners-wise.

"And, Tommy," his mom said warmly. "Nice to see you again."

Ryan wondered if she'd still be saying that if she knew that not so very long ago Tommy had been mere moments away from pounding her firstborn son into a thick, gooey paste.

"Hi, Mrs. Hardy," Tommy said, looking down at his plate. "Um, thanks for the sandwich."

Though Tommy kept his more antisocial tendencies in check at the Hardys' kitchen table, Ryan knew the most feared kid at Rod Serling Middle School wasn't going to become a warm and fuzzy person over one and a half peanut butter and jelly sandwiches and two glasses of milk. Though Ryan didn't quite fear him in the same way he had a few months ago, Tommy was not the Grinch and his heart had not grown three sizes since befriending Winston.

There was no telling any of this to Declan, however, who seemed inexplicably drawn to Tommy. At first he just stared at Tommy from his booster seat while he sucked all the apple juice from his sippy cup. Then he hopped down, toddled over, and started slapping Tommy on the thigh and raising his hands in the air.

"Hardy," Tommy said to Ryan. "What's he doing?"

"He wants you to pick him up," Ryan said.

"Why?"

"He likes you."

Tommy scowled down at Declan, then back at Ryan. "Why?"

Ryan shrugged. Tommy returned his attention to Declan, who was slapping Tommy's thigh again with unflagging determination.

"No," he said flatly.

HOME EARLY

Tommy was the one who spotted the car first.

It was a Monday, around five o'clock. About two weeks after Tommy and Winston had converted Ryan's garage into their secret art studio.

Tommy and Winston were with Ryan, Ernest, and Lizzy in the den watching TV.

"Hardy," Tommy said. "Your dad's home."

Ryan's dad hadn't been home before seven thirty in nearly two months. He and Mr. Wilmette were practically working around the clock on this bank prospectus. Since he'd gotten so used to not seeing his dad around while his friends were over, Ryan had forgotten about his earlier worries regarding Winston. But the flat tone in Tommy's voice brought them back in a hurry.

Ryan's dad came in through the front door to find his den crowded with kids, roughly half of whom were strangers to him.

"Hey, Dad," Ryan said cautiously as Declan hopped off the couch and hurled his little body onto his father's pant leg.

As Ryan's dad pried Declan off his thigh, Lizzy and Ernest waved and said hello. His dad's face unclouded a bit in recognition. Meanwhile, Winston rose from his seat and, just as he had done with Ryan's mother, extended his hand and introduced himself.

"Hello, Mr. Hardy," he said. "My name is Winston. Winston Patil."

Ryan felt a chill run through his veins as Winston's hand hung in the air. But it wasn't fear, or at least it wasn't the kind of fear he'd felt when he had faced down Tommy. Or even the fear Tommy felt about his own dad. It was the fear of never seeing his father in the same light again.

And maybe Doug Hardy saw that fear. Maybe he read in his son's eyes what the boy was thinking, and had been every day for the past several months. How his own anger had conditioned Ryan to steer clear of him. How he'd allowed weaker men into his TV, into his home, into his mind. Allowed them to frighten and agitate him, alter him. Make him less than himself.

Or maybe he just remembered who he really was.

"Hello, Winston," he said, taking the boy's hand firmly in his own. "Nice to meet you. I'm Doug Hardy, Ryan's father."

Mr. Hardy surveyed the room. "Where's Mom?" he asked.

Ryan said, "In the kitchen with Mrs. Wilmette."

"All right, then," Mr. Hardy said. "Anybody up for pizza?"

By the time the pizzas arrived, Lizzy's mom had finished work and come over to join them. It was a fun night, one of Ryan's all-time favorites. Because this was the night he got his father back. For the first time in longer than Ryan could confidently recall, he saw his dad joke around, and laugh, and smile. At one point Ryan's dad even made Tommy laugh. It was a deep laugh, a man's laugh, and it surprised everyone, even Tommy, who then laughed again at the sound of his own laughter.

In its own way, it was a perfect night. But it was also the night before everything began to fall apart.

17

GIRL CRUSH

"Class, today we have a special guest," Mr. Earle said, looking out his open door and into the hallway. "Her name is Andrea Chase and she's a television reporter."

Andrea walked into the room with broad, confident strides. She introduced herself and talked a little about her job. She told the class the places she'd been and the stories she'd covered. She said she was doing a piece on the Holyoke Red Diamond, and that she was in town looking for a fresh angle.

"Now, I noticed in several interviews Mr. Hought said that as a boy he'd gone to a local wishing well, Thompkins Well?"

Andrea Chase said searchingly. "Have any of you kids ever made any wishes at Thompkins Well?"

She may as well have just said, *Simon says everybody raise your hand and start talking all at once.*

Lizzy looked down and sank into her seat. Because it was all she could do to keep from raising her hand, too. Because although she knew better, Lizzy was dying to tell this woman everything. Andrea was beautiful and smart and successful. She was strong and confident, and Lizzy wanted the reporter to notice her, to like her.

Andrea Chase was a winner. Lizzy was positive there wasn't a man in the world who could make her cry.

Nevertheless, Lizzy could almost feel Ryan's eyes bearing down on the back of her head, telepathically shouting at her not to say a word about the well or the attic or, most of all, how they really found the sock monkey.

Lizzy held her tongue and was the first out the door when Mr. Earle dismissed them for lunch.

But then, at the end of the day, Mr. Earle caught her in the hallway.

"Lizzy, there you are. Do you have a minute?"

He led her into his classroom, where Andrea Chase was sitting on the edge of his desk.

When Lizzy entered the room, the reporter stood up and offered her hand.

"Hi, Lizzy," she said warmly. "We didn't get to meet personally earlier. I'm Andrea."

"Hi," Lizzy said nervously.

"I thought we could talk a bit, just one-on-one?" Andrea said. "Marcus here says you're one of his brightest students."

"Ever," Mr. Earle added.

"Ever, wow," Andrea said, impressed.

Lizzy blushed. "So, um, how do you know Mr. Earle?" she asked.

Mr. Earle and Andrea looked at each other and laughed.

"Right away with the tough questions. I think we might have a future journalist here, Marcus," Andrea said. "Well, Lizzy. The truth is that Marcus and I went to college together. We even dated a little," she said in a tone of mock scandal.

"You and Mr. Earle were boyfriend and girlfriend?" Lizzy laughed.

"You know," Mr. Earle said, his turn to blush now. "I think I'll just grab some coffee and leave you both to it."

After he left, Lizzy said, "How long were you guys . . ."

"About a year," Andrea said, a hard-to-read smile on her face. "He was sweet," she added in a way that was both affectionate and a little dismissive. "Anyway, the reason I wanted to talk to you, Lizzy, is that it's important for a journalist to find balance in a story. Do you know what I mean?"

"I think so," Lizzy said. "You want to make sure you cover all sides. That you don't just report on one point of view."

"Exactly," Andrea said. "Now, all the kids in your class today, they all really believed in this Thompkins Well business. That it grants wishes. And I have to admit, that girl with the brother who couldn't read and the Colorforms, that was pretty amazing. But I noticed you were . . . less than interested in the whole thing. Skeptical, perhaps?"

Lizzy shrugged, sensing these questions were going somewhere but not yet sure just where. "I'm not big on fairy tales," she said.

"Good girl," Andrea said. "We make our own happy endings, right?"

Lizzy smiled. It was like someone finally understood her. Saw things the way she did.

"The men who found the Holyoke Red Diamond," Andrea continued. "Mr. Hought and Detective Donan. Do you know them?"

Though it was asked in an offhand way, Lizzy knew there was weight behind this question.

"No," Lizzy said, looking away. "Never met them."

"Okay. Have you ever heard anything about them, though? Any, you know, small-town gossip? Anything like that?" Andrea gave her a just-between-us-girls smile that nearly made Lizzy blab the whole story right then and there.

"Sorry, no," Lizzy managed.

Andrea backed off after that. She started asking Lizzy if she might like to be a journalist herself someday, offering to help her along any way she could. Then Mr. Earle came back in.

"Safe to return?" he joked.

"Oh, I think so," Andrea Chase said, giving Lizzy a wink.

INCONVENIENCES

"What are you doing here?" Ernest's mom asked as she met him at the front door, going out just as he was coming in.

Ernest considered reminding her that he did live here, but she seemed harried and not in the mood.

"Ryan's mowing Mrs. Haemmerle's lawn today," he said instead. "So I figured I'd just come home."

Mrs. Wilmette frowned slightly the way parents do when kids have a perfectly reasonable answer that inconveniences them.

"Well," she said. "I have to go to Grandpa Eddie's house."

"Why?"

"I'm meeting with a realtor," she said. "We're putting Grandpa's house on the market."

A number of thoughts ran through Ernest's mind, most of them revolving around how he didn't want Grandpa Eddie's house to be sold, how he felt left out because his parents didn't tell him it was going to happen, and how this was just the latest in a growing list of important things his parents never told him.

But the one thought that rushed to the front of the line was this:

A realtor means a *For Sale* sign in the yard. It means open houses, and most of all, it means people coming into the house with the freedom to go anywhere they wanted.

Including the attic.

"Can I come along?" Ernest asked quickly.

WOBBLY, CALM, AND GETTING CLOSER

Aaron's eyes were getting wobbly on him. When you stare at a computer screen for long periods of time, it helps to look up every so often and focus on something farther away.

Aaron frequently forgot to do this.

He'd been going at it for weeks, ever since the day Jamie had so publicly mocked him and his footage from the woods. Aaron had isolated a five-second section that featured the mystery figure in question emerging from the woods and running past Aaron's camera.

There are thirty frames in an average second of video, but each one of those frames actually contains two images, which meant Aaron had a total of three hundred images.

So he started going through each one of those three hundred images, pixel by pixel, de-blurring and de-speckling so he could get a clean look at whatever was running out of the woods.

The meticulous, repetitive nature of the work would seem maddening to most people, but Aaron found it peaceful. Comforting, even.

In fact, ever since he had started on his project, Aaron had been calm. His legs didn't bounce when he sat down, not even at school, where he was often his most restless and bored. He wasn't clenching his jaw and his arms as much, either.

And to top it all off, he was pretty close to getting his answer.

CLEARING OUT THE ATTIC

Ryan had just finished Mrs. Haemmerle's front yard and was on his way to start the back when Ernest came over from across the street. He carried a grocery bag, and his eyes darted around furtively as he approached.

"Whatd'ya got there, Ernest?" Ryan asked as he emptied the clippings into a trash bag.

"My parents are selling Grandpa Eddie's house," Ernest said urgently. "My mom's meeting with the realtor right now."

"I know," Ryan said.

"You know?" Ernest said, incredulous.

"Yeah, I have to do the lawn this weekend. Full works: mow, trim, turn over the soil in the flower beds." Ryan caught how Ernest's face sagged. "I'm sorry, man. I thought you knew."

Ernest shook it off. "Anyway, there's no telling when I might be able to get back into the attic again, so I grabbed Rollo's last two presents."

Ernest reached down into the grocery bag. The first thing he pulled out was a quilt. It was a patchwork design, green and blue patterns sealed tight in thick plastic wrap. The second item was an old toy, a ray gun, still in its original packaging.

"Can I leave these with you?" Ernest asked.

"Sure," Ryan said, tying off the lawn trimmings. "Just put the bag in the garage and I'll bring it home with me when I'm done here."

"Thanks, Ryan," Ernest said, looking sadly across the street at his grandfather's house, a *For Sale* sign already in the front yard.

Ryan followed his friend's gaze. "Had to happen sometime."

"I guess so," Ernest said.

THE ACCIDENTAL ARSONIST

It wasn't Bigfoot.

Aaron had guessed as much a while ago, but knowing now for sure didn't upset him like he thought it might. After countless hours of rendering, the image was clear, or at least as clear as it was ever going to get.

The mystery figure wasn't Bigfoot; it was just some guy in a brown coat. An ugly brown coat, from what Aaron could make of it.

Aaron stared at the monitor for a few moments before he finally saw it. He could have kicked himself. All those hours and he hadn't put it together.

The hardest part had been digitally removing the smoke, pixel by pixel, to get at the figure underneath. All that time removing smoke and he'd completely overlooked the fire.

He thought he'd been looking at Bigfoot. But now he knew he was looking at a man. A man running out of a cloud of thick smoke.

Running away from a fire.

Running away from *his own* fire.

GOODBYE

To Ryan's surprise, Mrs. Haemmerle didn't come out to check on him while he did the lawn. In fact, except for a wave from the kitchen window when he first wheeled the lawn mower out of the garage, Ryan hadn't seen her at all.

By the time he'd finished and put the mower away, she still hadn't come out. Figuring she may have just fallen asleep, Ryan considered simply cleaning up and going home. But if he didn't even say goodbye, it might hurt her feelings. Or worse, it might confuse her, mess with her routine. He was already switching things around by doing her lawn on Tuesday, so as to free up the weekend to get the Wilmette lawn ready for the real estate showings next week.

Ryan went to the back door and knocked. When no one answered, he peered in through the kitchen window. Through the hallway he could see into the living room, where the reflection off the TV showed Mrs. Haemmerle asleep in her chair.

Something about the way she was slumped didn't look right.

The back door was locked, but Ryan knew Mrs. Haemmerle kept a key hidden in an empty flowerpot in the garage. Ryan unlocked the door, turned the handle slowly, and stepped inside. Though he'd been in this house a hundred times, he felt uneasy.

In the living room, Mrs. Haemmerle was still, very still. He looked for signs of breathing, but her chest didn't move at all. She drooped into the cushions, her arms tight to her sides, wrists crossed in her lap. Her mouth was open slightly, but it was taking no breath.

She looked cold.

Ryan's mind started buzzing—he had to call his mom, call 911—but first he had to do something about the cold.

He walked quickly through the kitchen and out the back door to the garage. There he grabbed the quilt out of the grocery bag and ripped off the plastic covering, oblivious to the boxed toy ray gun tumbling to the ground.

Ryan brought the quilt back and draped it carefully across Mrs. Haemmerle's body. He knew it didn't matter, that she was dead and couldn't feel warm or cold, or anything at all anymore.

But it mattered to Ryan. At that moment it was the only thing that did matter. He stayed with her a little bit longer, then went into the kitchen and picked up the phone.

After Ryan called his mom, she called Lizzy's mom, and both of them hurried over. The paramedics arrived and officially pronounced Mrs. Haemmerle deceased. They talked with the moms. Then Mrs. Hardy came over to him.

"Ryan, honey," she said softly. "The quilt on Mrs. Haemmerle. Did you put that on her after you found her?"

Ryan nodded. "Was that wrong?"

"No, not at all," his mom said. "How are you doing?"

Ryan nodded with little conviction and looked away. His mom put her hand on his back, rubbing it softly.

"It must have been a shock, finding her," she said. "A lot of kids—a lot of people—would have been scared finding someone that way."

"It wasn't that," Ryan said. "It's just . . ." He didn't want to say the next part but felt like it was going to jump out anyway. "She was all alone, Mom. She died alone."

He fell apart then, sobbing heavily, his whole body shaking with grief and frustration. For a long time his mom didn't say anything; she just held him close as he cried. But then, as he started to regain himself, she eased him away slightly so she could look him in the face.

"Ryan," she said tenderly. "I think you're wrong. Mrs. Haemmerle wasn't alone. She had you. She always had you."

Ryan wiped his face with his sleeve. "But I was outside."

"You may not have been in the room with her," his mom said. "But she knew you were here. When she sat down in that chair, when she closed her eyes and let go, what do you think was the last thing she ever heard?"

The piece-of-junk lawn mower, Ryan thought, and he had to smile.

"That's right," his mom said. "The sound of you taking care of her. She did not die alone, Ryan. You were with her."

AARON ROBINETTE AND THE CASE OF THE UGLY BROWN PARKA

Detective Art Dahl sighed the deep, heavy sigh of a man who had mistakenly thought the day's headaches were all squarely behind him. Then his son, Jamie, and that hyper Robinette kid came bursting into the den.

The boys were talking frantically and at once. Art told his son to be quiet and let Aaron talk. After some yammering about Bigfoot, the kid finally got to the point.

"Anyway, after running some image-enhancing software, I think I found something you might want to see, Mr. Dahl."

Aaron nodded to Jamie, who put a DVD into the player.

"Those are the woods by North Side Park," Jamie said. "The day they had that fire."

Art watched the footage. There was smoke and then, coming into frame, a figure.

In the ugliest brown parka ever made.

"Whoever this person is," Aaron said, "he's coming from the direction of the fire. I figured maybe he's the one who started it, or knows who did?"

"You filmed this yourself?" Art asked Aaron.

"Well, filmed isn't entirely accurate, since the recorder doesn't contain actual . . . I mean, yes, sir."

"And ran the software to sharpen the image? All by yourself?"

"Well, I had to know whether it was Bigfoot or not," Aaron said, as if this was the most obvious explanation of his actions.

"Is it a lead, Dad?" Jamie asked eagerly.

"Oh, it's more than that," Art said.

It was his nephew. Buddy. The idiot.

HARLAN BRICKS

Tommy Bricks was happy. And as an everyday state of mind, he still wasn't quite used to it.

Which was why Tommy didn't think very hard about the fact that he and Winston had knocked off early today. Winston's family was throwing a big party for his grandmother this weekend, and they had relatives flying in from Chicago.

But when Tommy got home he realized he had also not thought about the fact that his dad would still be there.

Tommy came in through the kitchen door and was halfway to his room when he heard his dad cursing a blue streak. Tommy thought about slipping down the hall and ducking into his room before his father noticed. But then he realized that his father was *in* his room.

"WHERE ARE THEY?" his father roared, kicking the box spring on Tommy's bed.

Tommy froze in the hallway just as his father stormed out of the room. Harlan Bricks wasn't a big man, but plenty of bigger men in Cliffs Donnelly gave him a wide berth. Years of working a factory line had given him lean, wiry arms and thick, weathered hands that could rip a phone book in half. To say he had a grip like a vise would be getting the metaphor backward. A vise, more accurately, had a grip like Harlan Bricks.

Tommy backed away, but his father reached out and grabbed him by the arm, squeezing hard as he pulled the boy closer.

"You have them, don't you?" he sneered.

Tommy tried to jerk his arm free. "What are you talking about?"

A darkness came over his father's face. "Sam's tools—where are they?"

"I don't have them," Tommy said, his eyes drifting across his ransacked bedroom. "Sam probably gave them to one of his friends before he left."

"Don't you lie to me," Harlan said quietly as he let go of Tommy's arm. He took off his belt and started folding it in half. "Do you have any idea how much money I could get for those tools?"

"I don't have them!" Tommy insisted, backing up slowly.

Harlan followed, smacking the belt against the wall as he

pointed at Tommy. "You're stealing, is what you're doing! Stealing from me. Stealing from us all!"

Tommy took off down the hallway.

He had just made it out the front door when Harlan caught up with him and shoved him off the porch steps. Tommy fell hard on the unforgiving dirt patch that passed for a front yard. Harlan hopped off the porch and stood over Tommy, swinging the belt back and across like a reaper. Tommy blocked the first couple of blows with his forearm but eventually had to cover his face, exposing his back to the belt.

Then it stopped. Tommy remained curled in a ball, eyes closed tight, as he heard his father gasping for breath overhead. He glanced up, hoping to see that Harlan had stepped away, that he was done.

But his father stood there, still looking furious as he slowly turned the belt over in his hands.

He's going to start swinging again, Tommy thought. Only this time with the . . .

"Harlan!" Tommy's mother shouted. "Are you crazy? Out on the front lawn?"

"He ran," Harlan said, winded.

"Of course he ran, you drunken fool," she said. "Put your belt back on."

Harlan squared his shoulders. "Don't you talk to me like that," he snarled.

Tommy's mother didn't move. She was a small woman but scary in her own way. She never forgot anything, never forgave anyone, could lie in wait as long as it took, and, well, everyone had to sleep sometime. Even a drunken fool like Harlan Bricks knew better than to cross her.

Harlan said, "What are you doing home?"

"Grabbing a shower and some food before I go back to finish my double."

After some cursing and dark promises, Harlan Bricks got in his car and drove off.

"You eat?" Tommy's mom said, looking down at him.

Tommy, still getting his breath back, shook his head.

"I'll reheat some sloppy joes," she said.

"Okay."

His mother started up the porch steps, then turned around. "Tommy," she said, not unkindly, "Sam's not coming back. And your father's not going away."

"WHAT YOUR TEACHER'S EX-GIRLFRIEND ISN'T TELLING YOU"

Lizzy rubbed her eyes. She had been on her mom's laptop all evening, learning everything she could about Andrea Chase.

The news wasn't good.

Andrea was an investigative reporter. Her specialties were takedown stories, attack pieces that fed on the audience's suspicions and fears. Lizzy watched a few of them. One segment was titled "What Your Pediatrician Isn't Telling You," and another was "So You Think You Can Trust Your Local Library."

Her stories were what's known as "yellow journalism." That was a kind of news reporting where keeping people interested by playing on their emotions (fear and anger, usually) was more important to the story than actually telling the truth. Exaggerating, distorting facts, misrepresenting situations—all that didn't matter as long as your story kept people watching.

And now Andrea Chase had set her sights on Cliffs Donnelly.

Lizzy couldn't believe she'd almost let herself trust Andrea. Even worse, Lizzy had actually wanted to be like her.

Worst of all, tomorrow Lizzy would have to tell Ryan and Ernest the truth about their friendly neighborhood reporter.

18

FAMILY COMMITMENT

"It's just for a couple of days," Winston said. "Through the weekend."

"Yeah," Tommy said. "You said that already."

Winston had hoped that his grandmother's birthday party wasn't going to completely disrupt his routine. But he was the oldest of three, and the minute his relatives started arriving from Chicago, his parents expected him to be home watching his siblings and playing host for pretty much every waking minute that he wasn't at school.

Now Tommy was doing that thing. Sometimes he got cold, distant, when he had something on his mind. He had moods.

Really dark moods. And he'd been in one all day. The worst thing would be to ask if he was okay. But that's precisely what Winston wanted to do, because he had a strong feeling that this time Tommy really wasn't.

"Your ride's here," Tommy said flatly, gesturing with his head toward the blue minivan that had just pulled up to the front of the school. Winston's grandmother, a tiny old woman barely visible in the passenger-side window, waved at Winston while his mom gave two quick toots on the horn.

"Um, okay," Winston said. "So, I'll—"

"Yeah," Tommy said.

As Winston stepped into the minivan, he snuck a look back at Tommy, standing alone in front of the school.

"All right, Winston?" his grandmother said, following his gaze. "Your friend there, does he want a ride?"

"No, Grandma," Winston said. "He doesn't."

HERE COMES THE FUZZ

Buddy was barely one foot outside the high school when he saw his uncle's dark blue sedan double-parked in the turnabout right in front of the building.

"Get in," Uncle Art called out. Buddy got in.

In the car, Buddy's uncle told him that he knew Buddy and his burnout friends had started that fire in the woods last month and that he better not try to deny it.

Buddy tried to deny it.

Uncle Art stopped in front of the fire station. "Deny it again and I'll lock you up for the night," he said, getting out of the car.

Uncle Art brought Buddy to the fire chief's office. The two men had clearly spoken already, because the minute the fire chief shut the door, they sat Buddy down and showed him some video of him running away from the fire in his telltale brown parka.

Buddy admitted that he started the fire. He explained how it all happened but wouldn't tell who was there with him. Uncle Art and the fire chief seemed to buy his story—it was the kind of dumb accident that fit nicely with his uncle's opinion of him. Uncle Art and the fire chief talked among themselves and decided to hand him over to someone named Julia.

Buddy had no idea who Julia was. But from the way the two men snickered, it didn't sound like he was off the hook.

LOCAL COLOR

Andrea Chase had been at North Side Park with her cameraman, Chuck, doing interviews all afternoon. Thompkins Well had become a local tourist attraction, and Andrea was having an easy time getting people to talk about it.

Andrea hated this part of the job, the local-color interviews, but they were what really sold the story. It was an easy crowd, friendly and talkative, and before long, Andrea and Chuck had piled up a half dozen solid interviews. If she played her cards right, she was going to get two stories on this trip for the price of one. Once she finished her takedown piece on the Holyoke Red Diamond, she could tear apart this Thompkins Well fairy tale for dessert.

She had doubted the Holyoke Red Diamond story from the very start. The way the diamond was supposedly discovered just didn't ring true to her. It was just too sweet, too cute, too hopeful not to be a lie.

What really sold her was the nonsense about the wishing well. The way the son of the thief had said that when he was a little boy he'd thrown a quarter in the town wishing well to learn the truth about what happened to his dad. That was the tell, the giveaway.

That's when she knew she really had something.

Because however much people love a feel-good story, they love *turning* on a feel-good story even more. Audiences may hunger for the warm fuzzies, but they get positively ravenous for an exposed lie.

Andrea had built her career on it.

When she then discovered that her old boyfriend was a teacher in the town, that she'd have an inside track on the local scuttlebutt, it was like fate. She couldn't have wished for a better setup.

And when Andrea first got to Cliffs Donnelly, she interviewed Jack Hought and Detective Donan. Hought had been evasive but mostly consistent with his story. Donan had played the addled old codger, scratching his head and fiddling with his hearing aid. He kept calling her Amy by accident and asking her to repeat her questions.

It was a good performance, but Andrea didn't buy it. Detective Donan looked too good. If the old man had really been as senile as he let on, his pants would have been wrinkled and there'd have been tapioca stains on his shirt.

He was hiding something.

It was a girl in Marcus's class who helped her put it all together. Lizzy was an awkward girl but clever, Andrea could tell.

She sat up front, her big, eager eyes glued on Andrea from the minute she walked in the door. At first the girl was on the edge of her seat, hanging on Andrea's every word, but then once Andrea got the other kids blathering about Thompkins Well, the girl's body language completely changed. She closed off, slumped down in her chair, and lowered her head. Like she was scared.

Andrea then spotted two other kids, boys, in different parts of the classroom. One, a small, bouncy kid, kept looking over at Lizzy and another, bigger boy. The other boy just stared straight ahead. Andrea's gut told her these three kids were connected. But the girl, Lizzy, she was the key.

So Andrea had asked Marcus to bring Lizzy to his classroom after school. The girl had almost cracked. Still, Andrea could definitely tell that she was lying when she said she didn't know Hought and Donan.

After her meeting with Lizzy, Andrea had gone back to Shady Lanes. It was almost too easy. Old people love to talk, and kids stand out at a retirement home. Andrea was there barely twenty minutes before she had confirmation that two boys and a girl had, indeed, visited Detective Donan on the very day that Donan and Hought discovered the Holyoke Red Diamond. Even better, a couple of residents actually recalled seeing the sock monkey. One lady had even loaned Detective Donan her seam ripper so he could open the stuffed animal and retrieve the diamond inside.

Of course there could be an innocent explanation for it all. But innocent, Andrea knew, was boring. And she didn't get paid to be boring.

As evening set in and the crowd thinned, Andrea and Chuck started to pack up and call it a night. Then a slight and unassuming boy entered the park and made his way straight for the well.

Andrea recognized the boy from Marcus's class. She remembered him because, like Lizzy and the other two boys, he took no part in the class discussion. At first Andrea thought he might be with the other three, but this boy spent the whole time staring out the window with a forlorn, faraway look in his eyes. He wasn't avoiding the discussion; he was ignoring it.

The boy stood quietly at the well for several moments. Andrea nudged Chuck, who had just laid his camera down in the back of the SUV. She mouthed silently, "Get this!" and pointed at the boy. Then they stayed back, partially hidden by the SUV as Chuck shot the boy standing at the well.

For a good half a minute the boy continued to just stand there, not making a sound, not moving a muscle. Then he said, quietly, "Last year my brother was killed in Afghanistan." He didn't say anything else for a few moments, then, in almost a whisper: "I . . . I just want my family back. Please."

"Tell me you got that," Andrea said once the boy had wandered out of earshot.

"I got it," Chuck said, checking his playback.

"And the audio. Please tell me—"

"I got it," Chuck said. "I got it all."

It was too good to be true. She could see it now. She'd air the sad little boy at the well, wishing for his dead soldier brother to come back, just before the commercial break. Then return with the one-two punch, how Cliffs Donnelly was home to not one, but two hoaxes. How all the hope, all the good feelings surrounding this town were nothing but lies. The audience would be outraged. They'd be furious. They'd eat it up.

Yeah, she could really work with this.

TOMMY'S HIDEOUT

At the far end of Rod Serling Middle School was a large storage room, about the size of a two-car garage, where Truman the Custodian stored a riding mower, weed whacker, hedge clippers, and other assorted groundskeeping equipment. And the only way in and out of the room was through a thick, metallic double door that was kept locked. But one of the doors was loose on its hinges, just enough so that most of the time the latch didn't quite catch.

Tommy Bricks knew this because he had scouted the storage room as a possible hiding place for Sam's tools back at the beginning of the school year. Though Tommy had ultimately decided against using it, now with his father home and Winston's extended family in town, he had something else he needed to hide for a little while.

Himself.

So after Winston drove away with his grandmother, Tommy went back behind the school and into the trails for about an hour.

Then, once Truman the Custodian had finished his rounds outside the school, Tommy emerged from the woods and slipped into the storage room.

And waited for it to get dark.

BLOWUP

"This is bad," Ryan said quietly.

They were in the Hardys' den. Lizzy had just shown the boys some of Andrea Chase's old TV segments. Then she told them about her little after-school meeting with Andrea, and how the reporter had asked her if she knew Mr. Hought and Detective Donan.

"But I didn't say anything," Lizzy insisted.

"It doesn't matter," Ryan said. "This is a woman who did an attack piece on public libraries. She's not going to stop till she gets the story she wants."

They were all quiet for a moment, and another few after that.

"Well, maybe—" Ernest began sheepishly.

"Maybe what?" Ryan snapped. The mere sound of Ernest's voice, the very gee-whiz essence of it, flipped a switch inside Ryan. "What, Ernest? What?!"

"Ryan, go easy," Lizzy said.

But Ryan was done going easy. Going easy was what had gotten them into this mess, and now they'd taken it all too far.

"Face it," Ryan said to Lizzy. "We're in big trouble. Sooner or later she'll connect us to the diamond, and Mr. Hought and Detective Donan. Once that secret is out, it will be easy for her to tell the story any way she wants. Maybe then she'll find the cave, or figure out that the diamond was really in Eddie Wilmette's attic for sixty years. Either way, it's just a matter of time before that reporter tracks everything back to us—three kids, hiding in the well and listening in on people's wishes. And then, just like that, the magic or miracles or luck or whatever you want to call it becomes a lie. A giant hoax."

"But it's not a hoax!" Ernest interjected. "You know that."

"If only that mattered," Ryan said. "But all that really matters is what the whole town is going to think."

"That we tricked them," Lizzy said.

"Exactly."

"That's not true," Ernest said. "Or at least it doesn't have to be."

Ryan was having none of it. Not now, not from Ernest. "Quiet," he said, giving Ernest a withering glare. "The grown-ups are talking."

Ernest recoiled. Ryan knew it was a cruel thing to say, but blurting it out made him feel better.

"Ryan, stop it," Lizzy said.

He didn't stop. "No. I'm sick of coddling him. I already have one pain-in-the-neck baby brother—I don't need another." And then, oddly enough, Ryan heard himself chuckling. "If only," he said quietly.

"What?" Lizzy said.

"If only," he said, louder. "Just another day in If Only, Ohio, right? As in: *If only* I hadn't introduced Ernest to Mrs. Haemmerle, or *if only* we hadn't ever gone inside Thompkins Well, or even better," and here he looked over at Ernest, "*if only* I had just let Tommy Bricks beat the snot out of him two months ago—"

"Ryan!"

"—then maybe none of us would be in this mess!"

Ernest ran out of the room. Lizzy followed, but not before stopping to give Ryan a look he would never forget. A cold, hard look of hurt and disappointment, a look you give someone who has really, really let you down.

19

REGRET, RESOLVE

Ryan spent the whole night lying in bed and thinking about it.

He had never been ashamed before. Sure, he'd screwed up plenty in his life, but until today he'd never done anything that made him truly think less of himself.

Those things he'd said to Ernest, they'd have been terrible to say to anybody. But saying them to Ernest was like kicking a puppy.

Ernest was his friend. Or, more likely, *was* his friend. Ryan wouldn't blame Ernest if he never spoke to Ryan again.

What made him the most ashamed, though, was that he'd let his fear get the better of him. He was scared. Scared of being found out and of what everyone would say when they learned he had been in the well. Ryan had let all that fear take over. He'd let it make him someone he didn't like at all.

But it had happened and there was no use dwelling on it. For now, he could only do two things: Promise himself never to let fear control him like that again, and figure out how to protect his friends, even if they didn't want to be his friends anymore. Otherwise, all those wishes would be undone. Every good thing that had happened these last couple of months would unravel, like a spool of thread. And then this town would be worse off than before.

This, Ryan realized, would be the worst of all outcomes. Worse, even, than getting caught.

At first he thought the answer lay in covering their tracks. They could make sure that no one could trace the well or Rollo's gifts back to them. But that, he realized, would really be half a solution.

The only way to stop Andrea Chase from controlling this story, from telling it however she wanted to, was to control it himself. And the easiest way to control a story is to give people someone to blame.

He'd learned that much from those news shows his dad always watched.

And when you looked at it like that, there was really only one thing to do.

2 MUCH 2 DAY

Ryan avoided them the next day at school. He wouldn't even look at them, and Lizzy couldn't believe it. After all the things he'd said yesterday, Ryan owed Ernest an apology to beat all apologies.

Ernest. The poor guy was inconsolable. He'd barely said a word at lunch. He just sat there, staring at his food while Lizzy tried, in vain, to cheer him up.

When the last bell rang, Lizzy considered going after Ryan and really giving him a piece of her mind. Maybe even punch him in the nose again. But this notion was drowned out by two insistent horn blasts from the parking lot, followed immediately by the caterwauling of an all too familiar and all too screeching voice.

"Lizzy! Gawd! C'mon!"

Lizzy looked over to see her cousin Chelsea leaning half-way out the passenger-side window of Aunt Patty's colossal SUV.

Lizzy pulled her phone out of her pocket. There was a text waiting from her mom.

Last minute shift at hospital. Sorry. Couldn't reach Mrs. Hardy.

Need u 2 go to ur cousins for the afternoon.

Love you :)

Lizzy dropped the phone back into her pocket. Just when she thought her day couldn't possibly get any worse—

More honking.

"Hurry up, you stupid cow!"

RYAN CLEANS UP

After school Ryan went straight to Mrs. Haemmerle's house. It was only mid-afternoon, but the sky was crammed with dark, heavy storm clouds that made it seem later.

Though he had finished cutting the grass before finding Mrs. Haemmerle, the lawn mower needed to be put away, the clippings bagged, and the bins brought out to the curb. There was some small trimming and edging to be done as well.

He had to make sure the lawn looked good, clean. It was his way of saying goodbye to Mrs. Haemmerle. And that he was sorry for what was to come.

Ryan made the chores last as long as he could, but finally there was no more to do. After he put the lawn mower back in the garage, he allowed himself one quick glance at the house. For a split second he was sure he saw a figure, a woman with long hair, passing by the kitchen window. Right where Mrs. Haemmerle would stand and wave at him to see if he was ready for a lemonade break.

At that exact moment a low rumbling pulled his gaze to the clouds opening up overhead. Then he glanced back at the window and shook his head. He tried to tell himself that the figure had been a trick of the eye.

But she'd been right there. He had seen her.

And then she was gone.

BAIT AND SWITCH

"This isn't a good idea, Andrea," Marcus Earle said slowly, deliberately. "That family has been through too much already."

Andrea had shown him the footage of Josh at the well, wishing for his family back. Now she wanted to go to the boy's house and interview him.

"I understand," Andrea said. "But maybe something like this would be good for the family. You said yourself this boy barely speaks in class."

"This is starting to sound a little self-serving, Andrea."

"That's not fair," Andrea said, a hurt look on her face. But she hadn't really wanted Marcus to help her with the Rediggers anyway. She was just putting him off balance before she asked him to help her get the story she was really after.

"Okay," she said. "I could maybe lose the footage of Josh at the well."

Marcus slumped in relief. "Thank you, Andrea."

"But I'm going to need your help with something else, Marcus."

ENOUGH

Chelsea was even pushier than usual today. Perhaps she sensed vulnerability, a weakening of resistance on Lizzy's part, and decided to see how far she could push her advantage.

"Ooh, I know," Chelsea said. "Let's do Lizzy's hair."

Amber's body stiffened; she gave a barely perceptible warning shake of the head in Lizzy's direction.

"Chelsea, I don't—" Lizzy began.

But Chelsea was already back from her mother's bathroom with various hair care products, most notably a dyeing kit.

"This is going to be awesome!" Chelsea squealed.

"No, it's not. We're not—"

"I'm thinking we go lighter, put some streaks in it maybe."

"Chelsea," Lizzy said firmly. "I said no."

Chelsea cocked her head, a confused and disturbed look on her face, as if Lizzy had just spoken in tongues. Then she sighed and dropped the hair products on the floor. "Fine," she said. Then, under her breath but not really, "Be a lonely old hag just like your mom."

That's it, thought Lizzy. I'm done with this.

Lizzy lowered her gaze and advanced on Chelsea, slowly but with a purpose that would not be altered. "Excuse me?" Lizzy growled in a voice not entirely her own. "What did you just say, you repulsive, bitter, obnoxious, tacky nightmare?"

Amber squeaked in fear (and, just possibly, a pinch of amusement).

For a split second, Chelsea looked like she might stand her ground. Then her lip started to tremble, her throat spasming like a turkey's gullet as she wailed, "MOOOOOOOOM!!!"

Lizzy didn't blink, didn't even flinch. So Chelsea followed her cry for reinforcements with a tactical retreat, nearly colliding with her mother on the stairs.

Lizzy sat down at the foot of the bed and waited. To her shock, she was completely at peace. And for the next moment or two, nothing mattered. Nothing at all. Because Lizzy felt relieved—and whole—in a way she hadn't for a long time now.

Amber, meanwhile, made the rather brave move of joining Lizzy at the foot of the bed, and sitting quietly beside her.

JUST A STORY

"Andrea, they're just kids."

"I know, but they're hiding something. Possibly something criminal." She had explained about her meetings with Hought and Donan, how their stories were sketchy, how they'd stone-walled her. She'd told Marcus that Lizzy lied about knowing Donan, and that the girl was seen at the retirement village with two boys from Marcus's class on the very day the diamond was discovered in the sock monkey.

"Everything you're saying is circumstantial," Marcus countered. "You still need facts. The truth of the matter is that you're just guessing."

"Truth? Grow up, Marcus. There is no truth. There's just *the story*: The story that people hear first, the story they hear most, and the story they like the best. If you can get two out of those three to be your story, that becomes the truth."

"You don't really mean that?"

"It's the way of the world, Marcus," she said. "Now, the story people hear first is usually the one they hear the most. And the story I tell will be the best."

Marcus slumped back against his desk, defeated. "They're just kids," he said again.

"I know, Marcus," Andrea said. "And we can protect them. We *will* protect them. I promise." She leaned forward then, cupping his face in her hands. "But to do that, I have to be first."

Marcus was quiet for a long time.

"Okay," he finally said. Then he started telling her everything she wanted to hear.

BUCKLE OUT

Truman the Custodian was moving slower today than he had yesterday, and it was close to dark before the coast was clear. By the time Tommy Bricks finally emerged from the woods, it had started to rain.

Five minutes after he slipped into the storage room, it was coming down hard. At first Tommy didn't mind. He'd found a can of Coke perched on the riding mower. It was still pretty cold. And though it was too dark to do any homework or sketch, he was warm, dry, and out of the storm.

But then the rain started coming down harder, and harder still. And that got Tommy thinking.

It's never going to let up. Not the rain. And not his father's rage. It's going to get worse. If nothing else, the other night proved that.

It wasn't the beating. Tommy had been on the end of his father's belt before. Well, that end of it.

The other night had been different, though. Because right before his mom showed up and stopped him, Harlan Bricks was turning the belt around.

Buckle out.

Tommy had seen it before, with Wade mostly, but also Sam. He'd seen what that buckle did to his brothers' backs. He'd seen the look it put in their eyes.

Laying low in the storage room had seemed shrewd at first. But it wasn't a solution. Just like Sam's tools, he couldn't keep hiding forever. The storm wasn't going away.

Sam wasn't coming back.

It hadn't sunk in at the time, but his mother was right. Tommy's brother wouldn't be coming home to save him.

Hidden behind his locker, along with Sam's tools, were the letters Sam had written to him ever since he left. Two letters a week, every week. And Tommy hadn't read a single one. He'd told himself it was because he was still mad at Sam for leaving. Now Tommy realized that wasn't it at all. He wasn't reading the letters because once he did, he'd know that it was true, that Sam was gone.

Tommy was strong. He knew how to survive, how to adapt. All his life he'd had to be tough in a way that most other kids, most adults, even, couldn't begin to understand.

But even Tommy Bricks had his breaking point. Now everything seemed utterly pointless. You can't wish away your lot in life. You can't fight what you are. You can pretend for a while, but . . .

When everyone expects the worst from you, sooner or later you're going to give it to them.

Tommy zipped up his hoodie and opened the door. It was coming down in sheets now, so hard there was a layer of mist hovering over the ground from the force of the dense rain crashing onto the asphalt.

It didn't matter. Nothing did anymore. Tommy was done hiding, done trying, done caring. Just done. He'd walk home in the cold and rain and if he got sick, if he got hit by a car, if his father was still home and beat him when he stepped through the door, so be it. He'd just close off the side of himself that hurt, that dreamed, that hoped. And he'd never look back.

Then, just before he stepped out into the consuming storm, he saw them.

Headlights.

They were coming up the main road and inching slowly, searchingly toward the school. As they got closer Tommy could make out that they belonged to a minivan. Winston's minivan.

When it reached the front of the school, Tommy saw that Winston's grandmother was driving.

The minivan passed the roundabout at the school entrance and pulled into the teacher's parking lot, where it finally stopped at the curb by a small pavilion of four covered picnic tables. The elder Mrs. Patil parked the car and got out. A tiny, wrinkled little woman, she walked purposefully to the covered tables with two bulging grocery bags of food. Winston got out of the passenger side, clumsily opened a massive golf umbrella, and scurried Tommy's way.

Tommy stepped out of the storage room to meet him.

"Winston?" he said. "What are you doing here?"

Winston's grandmother called to them. Tommy looked over and saw that she had laid out a picnic for them on one of the tables.

"Dude," Winston said. "You cannot believe how desperate I was to get out of that house."

20

NO APOLOGY

"Well?" Aunt Patty glared impatiently at Lizzy.

"Well, what?" Lizzy said in a low, even tone.

Aunt Patty blinked as if Lizzy had just flicked water in her face. "I think," she said slowly, a hint of menace in the back of her throat, "that you owe Chelsea an apology."

"And it better be good!" Chelsea insisted with a haughty lift of the chin.

Lizzy and her aunt shared a brief, awkward moment of confusion as to which of them Chelsea was actually addressing with this demand, before Lizzy said, "She's the one who owes me an apology. She called my mother a lonely hag."

Aunt Patty shot a quick, almost scolding glance in Chelsea's direction. Not necessarily for saying something cruel and hurtful, but rather for betraying a privately shared opinion in front of unwanted company.

"Lizzy," Aunt Patty said after a long, dramatic breath. "You need to understand something. You are a guest here, and as a guest—"

"That's right, Aunt Patty," Lizzy cut in. "I am a guest. I'm not a pet or a doll or a servant or a conversation piece to talk about as if I'm not here and don't have ears or feelings. I'm your *guest*. That means I shouldn't have to sit quietly while she, or *you* for that matter, trash-talks my mom for being a working single parent. But if I'm asking too much, if you can't do the bare minimum to make me feel even marginally welcome in your house, then for the good of us all, Aunt Patty, TAKE ME HOME!"

FETCH, BUDDY, FETCH

Uncle Art dropped Buddy off at the hospital, delivering him to Head Nurse MacComber, the Julia that his uncle and the fire chief had decided would be Buddy's punishment for starting the fire in the Nature Preserve.

"Nurse MacComber owns you now," his uncle said. "As long as she's happy, you and I are square. Follow me?"

Buddy followed.

After Uncle Art left, Nurse MacComber found Buddy a scrub shirt and temporary ID clip, and explained that he'd be tasked with any errand or chore that didn't directly involve patients, sharp objects, or Schedule II pharmaceuticals. For the next few hours, he fetched coffee, straightened up the waiting areas, took out the trash, fetched more coffee, organized the supply closet, and fetched even more coffee.

Nurse MacComber ran the ER, but she was quick to loan Buddy out to any of the nurses on other floors of the hospital. After one hour, Buddy was beat. After two hours, he was exhausted. By hour three, he realized he hadn't had a clue what exhaustion really felt like.

Then Nurse MacComber got a call and had to leave suddenly for a family emergency or something. This created a little confusion among the other nurses as to who should step in to order Buddy around. Desperate for a smoke, he slipped away from the ER but got turned around on his way outside and found himself wandering by the maternity ward.

He stopped to get his bearings in front of the heavy glass security doors that separated the viewing area from the rest of the hospital. Looking for an exit, his eye instead caught the rows of sleeping newborns on the other side of the glass.

"Hi there." It was a woman's voice, direct but friendly.

Buddy turned around. "Um, hi," he said. Then, pointing at the ID clipped onto his scrubs, he added, "Buddy."

The woman, a neonatal nurse, looked at the ID. "Well, hello, Buddy. I'm Jeanne." She gave Buddy an appraising look, one he was sure would result in the unspoken but familiar conclusion that he was an idiot. But instead she smiled at him and said, "You like babies?"

"Honestly, I never gave them much thought before."

Jeanne considered for a moment. "Come with me," she said.

RYAN'S PLAN

Ryan knew one way or another Andrea Chase would link them to the Holyoke Red Diamond. And from there to the attic, Thompkins Well, and the cave. She wouldn't stop until she had her story, until she had somebody to blame.

That somebody, Ryan had decided, would be him.

After dinner he grabbed his duffel bag from his closet and slipped out the window while his mom was putting Declan to bed. It was raining outside, hard in that way that means it won't be letting up anytime soon.

As Ryan jogged down the street, he heard thunder in the

distance. When he reached Grandpa Eddie's house, he snuck up the side opposite the driveway and hopped a low fence into the backyard.

The first step was to break into Grandpa Eddie's house.

The second step was to call the police and report that someone had just broken into Grandpa Eddie's house.

The third step was to go into the attic and wait for the police to catch him.

The fourth step was where it got a little complicated. With his duffel bag full of whatever was left in the attic, Ryan would make a confession. He would tell the police he'd been stealing things from Eddie Wilmette's attic and hiding them in Mrs. Haemmerle's garage. His plan, he would say, was to sell the items online, where collectors would pay big money for sixty-year-old junk like they did on the antiques shows his mom liked to watch.

Even that part, Ryan suspected, would be easy enough. Getting the cops to believe a South Side kid was a thief wouldn't exactly be a tough sell, especially when they caught him red-handed in the attic. It was the next part that had to be played just right.

Ryan would have to convince the police that Mrs. Haemmerle had been getting senile, very senile. That would explain why he could hide all the stolen goods in her garage. But then one day, he'd say, he went to check on his stash and discovered it was all gone.

The trick would be to lead the cops into making the connection on their own, adding her senility to the stolen loot. He'd complain about what a loon she'd become shortly before her death and wonder aloud what she did with his stash. This was the part, even more than taking a false rap for burglary, that really didn't sit well with him. But one thing would lead to another and the cops would conclude that she was the one who left the Colorforms in the library, the fire extinguisher in the woods, the sock monkey in Jack Hought's house.

It wasn't a perfect story, and certain parts of it didn't really add up if you thought about it too much. But it would be enough. People would want it to be enough.

And no one would know about Ernest or Lizzy. Or the well.

THE HEALING POWER OF FOOD

There was a ton of food and Tommy didn't recognize any of it. Winston's grandmother poured each of them a cup of sweet tea out of a huge thermos and then set about preparing the plates. As she worked she explained, through Winston, what each dish was and how she made it when she was a girl back in her old neighborhood in India.

Winston handed Tommy a paper plate with what looked like a slider on it.

"This is called *vada pav*," Winston said. "Basically a fried potato patty in a bun. They call it the Indian burger."

Tommy took the plate quizzically. It looked unlike any food he had ever had before. But, then again, he'd never been a big fan of most of the food he usually ate anyway. So when Winston's grandmother ordered Tommy (through Winston) to eat, he ate.

It was the best meal of his young life. He had three of the burgers and then a lentil and rice dish called *khichdi*. For dessert Winston's grandmother gave them rice pudding and peanut butter cookies (which she'd never made as a girl back in India, but were Winston's favorite).

Like a lot of kids with Tommy's kind of home life, he had learned at a young age how to size up people quickly. He knew Winston's grandmother could speak English but was using a perceived language barrier to make it harder for Tommy to resist her commands. And he also knew that the food they were eating wasn't just any food. This was working-class food. This was tortillas and rice, ratatouille, a bologna sandwich on white bread. This food was special to Winston's grandmother; it was her food.

It was still raining when they finished eating. Winston offered him a ride home. Tommy declined. Winston looked worried his grandmother might insist, but Tommy knew she wouldn't. She got it.

Instead, Mrs. Patil berated her grandson in Marathi for never bringing his friends around to the house. The little old woman then walked back to the minivan, giving the vehicle a disapproving once-over and muttering something else in Marathi (loosely translated, it was "I still miss driving my Ambassador") as she opened the driver-side door.

Tommy watched the minivan disappear into the night before he went back into the storage room. He left the door open so he could watch the rain.

It could go on all night, he thought.

But that wouldn't be so bad. Because he wasn't hiding now. He was just waiting out the storm.

A CROWDED BURGLARY

Breaking in had been a pretty good plan. There was just one problem: Someone had beaten him to it.

Once in Eddie Wilmette's backyard, Ryan had started to circle the house, checking the first-floor windows, when he spotted something.

There were two people already inside the house, lurking around in the dark.

What the . . . A real burglary was upstaging his fake burglary!

Ryan's first thought was to run back home and call the police. But his house was too far down the block.

He looked across the street at Mrs. Haemmerle's. He still had the spare key to her house from the flowerpot; he could call from there.

Ryan ran across the street, up Mrs. Haemmerle's driveway, and into her backyard. Drenched, he slipped inside and headed for the kitchen. He picked up the old phone on the wall and was just about to dial when he caught sight of a figure reflected in the kitchen window. Ryan spun around.

It was her. The woman with long hair. The rain on the window had made her look blurry the last time he'd seen her, and now the darkness of the room was making her equally hard to discern. He could barely tell if she was really there.

In the next few seconds a lot of thoughts raced through Ryan's mind. This woman looked like Mrs. Haemmerle, only much younger. Which led to the natural conclusion that he was standing in the kitchen with Mrs. Haemmerle's ghost. Though he *had* been operating on very little sleep or food for the last day and a half. Ryan didn't believe in ghosts, but that thought failed to get any traction.

He backed away toward the door just as a bolt of lightning cracked the sky and illuminated the woman who now stood in front of him.

"Ryan?" she said, her voice soft and almost otherworldly.

And then he fainted.

BABY CLAIRE

After washing their hands for what seemed like forever, Jeanne brought Buddy into the neonatal ICU. There was only one baby in the unit, a tiny girl inside a clear plastic incubator.

"Why is she in there?" Buddy asked quietly.

"She was born premature."

"You mean too early?"

"That's right," Jeanne said. "So we put her in there to help her. It's kind of like she's still in the womb."

Buddy walked over to the incubator and read the tag on the side. The girl's name was Claire. She was so small and fragile she almost didn't look real. "Is she going to be okay?"

"She has a good chance," Jeanne said. "She's a fighter."

Jeanne grabbed a nearby chair and pulled it up alongside the incubator. "Sit," she said to Buddy.

He sat, now eye level with baby Claire. She was awake, but her eyes were heavy, as if she wasn't sure whether to go back to sleep or not.

"Put your hand through that little hole there," Jeanne said, gesturing.

"Really?"

"Newborns need all the physical contact they can get." She

took his hand. "Here," she said. He put his hand through, his finger brushing Claire's tiny palm.

Instinctively the infant's thin little digits curled around Buddy's index finger. He gasped in surprise.

"Pretty cool, huh?" Jeanne said.

". . . Yeah," Buddy said.

"All right, then," she said, heading for the door. "I'll come back and check on you two in a little while."

"Wait!" Buddy said, softly but urgently. "I mean, what do I do?"

Jeanne shrugged. "Talk to her. Let her hear your voice. Just . . . be with her."

Buddy felt awkward, scared, and angry in quick succession, but the more he looked at baby Claire, the more he felt resolved. He wasn't leaving.

He wasn't talking yet, either. Whatever he said was just bound to be stupid.

But he could sing. He remembered a really old song his mom used to sing to him when he was little. How did it go, again? Oh, yeah.

> *"You say it's only a paper moon*
> *Sailing over a cardboard sea*
> *But it wouldn't be make-believe*
> *If you believed in me . . ."*

TESS

When Ryan came to a few minutes later, he was on the floor, his feet elevated and a little pillow under his head. The kitchen lights practically blinded him, but soon his eyes focused on the young woman standing over him. And there was a man next to her.

It was . . . Mr. Earle?

He smiled down at Ryan. "You okay there?"

Ryan nodded slowly as Mr. Earle helped him to his feet. He led Ryan to a small kitchen table and sat him down.

"I was . . ." Ryan started. Wait, what was he doing? What with the fainting and the ghost of Mrs. Haemmerle and the burglars—wait, the burglars!

"The Wilmette house," he blurted out. "Someone's robbing it. Now!"

"Way ahead of you," Mr. Earle said, smiling mischievously at the woman. Then, noticing Ryan's confused look, he said, "Oh, I'm sorry, Ryan. This is Tess Haemmerle. Mrs. Haemmerle's granddaughter."

Tess smiled warmly, as if she already knew him, and offered her hand. "Hi, Ryan. My grandmother mentioned you often. She was very fond of you."

ERNEST IS FED UP

"I don't understand," Ernest's mom said quietly into the phone.

Ernest had been in the room when she'd answered her cell. It was his dad, and whatever he was saying had taken the air right out of her.

"I can't believe it," she said, listening more than talking. "Okay. I will." And she hung up.

"What's wrong?" Ernest said.

His mom leaned against the kitchen counter, her hand cradling her forehead. "Nothing, honey," she said absently.

"Mom, it's clearly not nothing."

She looked up at him with an expression of strained patience that said, *Please, child, not right now.*

"Tell me," Ernest pressed.

"Ernest, you don't need to worry about it."

"Don't say that!"

He knew this was the time to really lay it all out there—the secrets, the sheltering, the overprotectiveness, the stupid back seat—but the only thing he could get out was "I am not a baby, Mom!"

Of course, it's categorically impossible not to sound like a baby when you're telling your mom that you aren't one. Ernest realized as much as soon as the words came out of his mouth, and promptly ran out of the kitchen.

His mom called after him as he flew through the front door and down the street. She called after him again from the front steps, but Ernest, who was fed up with his parents, fed up with his friends, fed up with the well, fed up with himself, just kept running.

21

MR. EARLE IS UP TO SOMETHING

Tess and Mr. Earle brought Ryan to the big bay window in Mrs. Haemmerle's living room. Looking through it was like having a front-row view of the Wilmette house, which now had two police cruisers, lights flashing in the rain, parked out front.

At first Ryan panicked, thinking they were looking for him. But then he remembered that he hadn't actually broken into the house. "I don't understand."

"Wait for it," Mr. Earle said.

The front door opened and a police officer stepped out, leading a handcuffed Andrea Chase. She was not happy.

"That's your reporter girlfriend."

"Former girlfriend," Mr. Earle clarified. Then, with a look toward Tess, "Very former."

Ryan's brows furrowed. They were sharing that moony look two people give each other in the movies so you know they're falling in love. But there was something else behind it as well. Something . . . What was the word . . .

"Conspiratorial!" Ryan blurted out.

"Come again?" Mr. Earle said.

Ryan understood what was happening here, but he was still having trouble working it out. "You two," he said, pointing out the window at the arrest in progress. "You guys made that happen."

THE BEST STORYTELLER IN CLIFFS DONNELLY

Andrea Chase had been right when she said that Marcus Earle was sweet. But he was something else, too.

Marcus Earle was a storyteller.

And a couple of hours ago, he had told her a doozy.

The previous evening Marcus Earle had gone to the Columbus airport to pick up Tess Haemmerle, who had just flown in from San Francisco to begin making the funeral arrangements for her grandmother. Marcus and Tess had been close friends in high school, and on the hour drive from Columbus to Cliffs Donnelly, she gave him the inside scoop on her grandmother's little sock monkey adventure, which just happened to involve three of his favorite students.

So when Andrea showed up in his classroom and ambushed him with her distorted but not entirely baseless conspiracy theories, Marcus Earle was ready to tell her what she wanted to hear.

"It's . . . it's bigger than you realize, Andrea," he'd started. "This goes back three generations, and it could affect the whole town."

Andrea got out her tape recorder, but Mr. Earle shook his head vehemently. "There can't be any proof that I told you what I know about the Holyoke Red Diamond."

Andrea nodded and handed over the tape recorder to prove it was off.

Mr. Earle continued, "Ben Mattingly didn't work alone."

"I know. He worked with Orson Muldoon out of Chicago."

"No, Muldoon was just the buyer. He was a criminal, but he wasn't Mattingly's fence."

"Okay, so who was Mattingly's fence?"

"Edgar Wilmette."

"*Edgar Wilmette?* As in Wilmette Stamping, Tool & Die?"

"You know how you said Lizzy was at the retirement home

with two boys? One of those boys was Ernest Wilmette, Edgar Wilmette's great-grandson."

Andrea gasped. "So Edgar Wilmette and Ben Mattingly . . ."

"Were partners in crime? Yeah," Marcus said.

Andrea was catching on. "He used his factory to launder the money they made from Mattingly's heists."

"And he used his house to hold all the loot from those heists," Marcus added.

Andrea's eyes lit up. "That's it! That's the cover-up. Jack Hought couldn't have found the sock monkey among his mother's old things because it was hidden in the old Wilmette house all this time!"

"Right. Edgar Wilmette had kept it all hidden in his house. The house he bequeathed to his son, Eddie Wilmette, who lived there until *he* died, a few months ago."

"And that's where the kids come in, isn't it? They found the Holyoke Red Diamond."

Mr. Earle nodded. "There is a false wall covering an old coal room in the basement. It's still filled with all kinds of jewels and money from Mattingly's old heists."

"You're kidding! But how did your students find it? Did Eddie Wilmette tell them?"

Mr. Earle shook his head. "No. I really don't think he ever knew about it."

Andrea looked perplexed. "Then how would the kids know to

even look for the room? Someone else had to have been helping them."

She looked stumped for just a moment, and then the penny dropped. "Edgar Wilmette and Ben Mattingly had a third partner, didn't they?"

Mr. Earle nodded. "They needed someone to provide protection."

"Detective Stanley Donan!" Andrea said. "He was the third partner!"

"Right. Up to a point."

"You mean, he turned on Wilmette and Mattingly?"

"I mean that Orson Muldoon didn't kill Ben Mattingly."

Andrea gasped. "Stanley Donan did!"

Marcus Earle nodded ruefully. "Ambushed him in Chicago the day after Mattingly stole the Holyoke Red Diamond. But Mattingly had already sent the diamond to Edgar Wilmette inside the sock monkey. Donan couldn't go after Wilmette: He was untouchable in Cliffs Donnelly. Still, he always knew the diamond was hidden somewhere on the Wilmette property. After Edgar Wilmette died, Donan tried to buy the house from Eddie Wilmette, but Eddie wouldn't sell."

"Then Eddie dies and Donan sees his chance."

"Yep. He makes Eddie's grandson, Ernest, do the looking for him. Threatens Ernest and his friends if they don't help him find the diamond."

"Then he returns the diamond to the Holyoke Foundation and collects the reward." Andrea shook her head in amazement. "And Lizzy told you all of this."

"She did. After you started asking questions."

"And you haven't gone to the police?"

"How could I, Andrea? Donan might still have friends on the force. Who knows how high up this goes?" Mr. Earle just shook his head. "No, better to just give the old man what he wants."

"He's a murderer, Marcus!"

"All the more reason!" he shot back, panic in his voice. "Look, I don't care about diamonds or jewels or cash or whatever happened sixty years ago. I just want those kids safe."

"And they will be," Andrea Chase said, grabbing her bag and making for the door. "Trust me."

She was off like a shot.

STANDING IN THE FOYER

Lizzy had been standing in the foyer with her backpack for the last twenty minutes. Though Aunt Patty probably wanted Lizzy out of her house just as much as Lizzy did, she wasn't going to make it easy for either of them. So instead, she told

Lizzy to wait there, went into the kitchen, and called Lizzy's mom.

Finally, the doorbell rang. Aunt Patty marched into the foyer without so much as a backward glance at Lizzy and opened the door.

Lizzy's mother stepped through the doorway. When she spoke, she didn't even look at Lizzy. She just said in a quiet voice, "Go wait in the car."

RYAN HAS A LOT TO PROCESS

"So you knew she'd try to break in and find the loot?"

"I figured that if I could convince her that Stanley Donan was a dirty cop, then she wouldn't go to the local police for fear that he still had allies in the department. That left finding the stash room herself."

Ryan worked that through. "Okay," he said. "I get that. But how did you know about me and Ernest and Lizzy, and how we really found the diamond in the sock monkey? That much was mostly true."

Ryan followed Mr. Earle's gaze over to Tess.

"Nana and I talked on the phone at least a couple of times a week. She told me all about it."

"So Miss Chase breaks into the house to find a stash room that doesn't exist while you guys are sitting here waiting to call the police on her," Ryan said, getting it straight in his head. "Man, you totally played her, Mr. Earle."

For the briefest of seconds Ryan's teacher betrayed a smile that was, almost, a little wicked. "No one messes with my kids, Ryan."

Ryan looked back out the window. Andrea Chase sat in the back seat of one of the cruisers as the cops led out some angry guy with a digital camera.

"So, Ryan," Mr. Earle said. "Maybe now you should tell us just what *you* were doing tonight."

DR. SHAY

Lizzy stepped outside and saw a black Mercedes sedan parked where she'd expected to find her mother's car. And standing by it, under an umbrella, was a tall, distinguished-looking man in a suit.

"Hello, Lizzy," the man said, extending his umbrella to cover her as well. "I'm Dr. Shay. I work with your mom." He offered his hand. "You can call me Tom," he added. "If you want."

Lizzy took his hand warily. This guy had to be someone

from the hospital. Did this mean her mom was in trouble for leaving work?

"Tom," Lizzy said. "Are you going to fire my mother?"

Dr. Shay gave her a funny look and then laughed. It was a big, booming roar that startled Lizzy. "Wow. I don't even know how to begin to answer that." He thought for a moment. "Okay, well, first of all, your mom doesn't work for me. I'm a cardiac surgeon and we do work together at the hospital, but I'm not her boss."

"So she's not going to get in trouble over this?"

"Lizzy, I'm not here in a work-related capacity," he said, fidgeting a little with his tie. "Your mom called me because . . ." He paused, thinking of the best way to say it. "Well, because she was too angry to drive."

He chuckled then, which confused Lizzy. Then it occurred to her that Dr. Shay was answering her questions in the way adults do when they want to remain technically honest but not entirely forthcoming.

"Wait a minute," Lizzy said, suddenly a little less confused. "Are you two dating?"

"Yes," Dr. Shay said very slowly. He looked like he was about to say more, but seemed relieved when the front door opened and Lizzy's mom marched out. Lizzy saw her aunt Patty standing in the doorway, trembling with the singular rage that comes from badly losing a verbal altercation.

When Lizzy's mom reached the car, she closed her eyes and

took a long, slow, cleansing breath. Then she folded Lizzy's hand in her own and smiled.

"I don't know about you two," Lizzy's mom said, brushing some of the rain out of her hair. "But I could just murder a cheeseburger right now."

RYAN TELLS HIS STORY

Ryan told Mr. Earle and Tess everything, starting with Winston and Tommy in the lunch yard. Then he told them about him and Ernest finding the little cave in the woods that led to the bottom of Thompkins Well. And what happened with the art set and the Colorforms. And the fire extinguisher. And finally the sock monkey with the jewel inside.

Then he told them about the quilt, and finding Mrs. Haemmerle. That part was hard.

Mr. Earle and Tess didn't say anything. They didn't once interrupt, not even to ask questions. Ryan could see on their faces that they weren't sure what to make of his story, but they believed him. Or at least believed he wasn't lying to them.

"After the sock monkey and the reporters, things started to get quiet again; we thought it was all done. But then your girlfriend—"

"Very former girlfriend. A lifetime ago."

"She showed up and wanted to . . . What's the word for proving something's fake?"

"Debunk," Tess offered.

"Yeah, that's it. She wanted to debunk the well and make everyone look like idiots for believing in it. If she'd succeeded, sooner or later everyone would know we'd listened to their wishes and think everything that happened was all a hoax, a prank. That none of it was real. But it *was* real. And even if it wasn't, Ernest only ever wanted to help people . . ."

He trailed off, thinking maybe he could stop there. But he wasn't finished, and they all knew it.

"Then I remembered how in class you were teaching us about scapegoats. And I realized that's what we needed. So I figured if I got caught inside Ernest's grandfather's house, everyone would just make me the scapegoat. And maybe there was a way to be the scapegoat and keep the miracle at the same time. People do like happy endings, as long as someone pays for them."

"Really, Marcus," Tess said. "What are you teaching these children?"

"So I'd say I stole all the stuff—the art set, Colorforms, all of it—and that I hid it in Mrs. Haemmerle's garage. Everyone buys that, because it's easy enough. Then I say that Mrs. Haemmerle, who was, no disrespect, getting a little senile, found my stash and started spreading it all over town."

"So you're the villain and she's the accidental hero."

"Pretty much."

Mr. Earle looked like he didn't know what to say. "That's very clever, Ryan. Very shrewd. Incredibly noble. And unbelievably stupid—"

"Hey! If I had known *you* already had a plan to get rid of your nosy girlfriend—"

"Very very *very* former nosy girlfriend! And if you had come to an adult for help—"

"Like you?"

"Well, sure. Me or—"

"Why, so you can call me stupid?"

"—or your parents, or Lizzy's mother, or—"

"She wasn't senile," Tess interjected, surprising Ryan and Mr. Earle. "My grandmother, she wasn't senile." She looked at Ryan and smiled warmly. "I know, Ryan. I know she never paid you. You always told her that she already had, but she knew the truth. She always knew."

THE PROBLEM WITH DRAMATIC EXITS

The problem with dramatic exits is that they happen so quickly a person rarely stops to consider the weather. Four blocks away from his house, Ernest was winded and coming down from the rush of adrenaline that had carried him this far, and he arrived at two key observations: (1) It was raining, and (2) it was cold.

What he wouldn't give to have his windbreaker right about now. As soon as he thought about it, he felt his stomach drop. Where was his windbreaker?

Come to think of it, he hadn't seen it for a few weeks now. There'd been a warm spell and he hadn't been wearing it to school. He tried to remember the last time he'd worn it, but all he could think of were those times he wore it to Thompkins Well, and how he kept forgetting it inside the cave.

What if it were in there now? And what if someone like that Andrea Chase discovered the cave and found his windbreaker?

With his name written inside it.

Ernest started running to North Side Park. He forgot about being cold and wet. He had to get to the cave. He had to get that windbreaker back before it was too late.

IRONY WITH A SIDE OF FRIES

Dr. Shay had gone up to the counter to pay the bill.

"I know, I know," her mother said before Lizzy could speak. "I should have told you."

"Then why didn't you?" Lizzy asked, more curious than upset.

Her mother shrugged sheepishly. "I was worried how you might take it."

And just like that, Lizzy realized how wrong she'd been about her mother—about everything—since her father had left. She hadn't been seeing her mother clearly at all.

Lizzy's natural instinct was to blame Aunt Patty and Chelsea (about whom her mother hadn't said one word all night, and wouldn't for another four days) for making her think less of her mother since the divorce, for letting their opinion sway her into believing that her mother wasn't pretty or feminine or strong enough to keep a man.

But Lizzy realized that what had actually set her off this afternoon was that she was mad at herself. Aunt Patty and Chelsea had been horrible, sure, but Lizzy was the one who had let them in her head.

Someone once famously said, "It's not what they call you; it's what you answer to." For the last several months, Lizzy had been answering to whatever her aunt and her cousin called her. Even worse, she'd been answering for her mom, too.

But she had it all wrong. Lizzy could finally see what she had been missing the whole time. Her mom didn't lose her dad. She got rid of him. Lizzy had assumed that her mom had wanted him back. But that wasn't why her mom cried at night. It was because he wouldn't come back for Lizzy.

"You really like him?" Lizzy asked. "Dr. Shay?"

Her mom looked at her. "I really do," she said with an unspoken question in her voice.

"Okay, then," Lizzy said. "Good enough for me."

TESS JINXES IT

"She knew you cut her lawn for free. And took care of her trash bins. And shoveled her walk. And more. And that every week you'd trick her into not paying you. She thought the world of you, Ryan. In fact, she . . ." Tess stopped herself, changing gears. "Well, that's a conversation for another time. Right now I think we should enjoy the present moment, yes? I mean, with Marcus's babe out of the picture—"

"Years and years—oh, forget it."

"—Ryan and his friends appear to be in the clear."

Ryan and Mr. Earle looked at each other. She had a point.

"There is just one more thing," Mr. Earle said after some careful thought. "By now your parents are probably wondering where you are. What are we going to tell them?"

Together, Ryan and Mr. Earle decided on a story that stuck pretty close to the truth. Leaving out Ryan's thwarted break-in, they would say that Ryan went back to Mrs. Haemmerle's to make sure he'd put the gas can for the mower back in the garage, at which time he noticed the burglary in progress across the street. Slipping into Mrs. Haemmerle's house to call the police, he came across Tess and freaked.

"Do we have to say *freaked*?" Ryan asked.

"Would you prefer *fainted*?"

Ryan shook his head.

Mr. Earle made the call and delivered the story. Ryan's mom was very anxious and worried but turned understanding and grateful once Mr. Earle, who really did spin a convincing yarn, finished his account.

He was just about to wrap up with her when she asked him to hold while she answered the door. A few moments later she came back on the line.

Mr. Earle listened, then turned to Ryan. "Mrs. Wilmette just came to your house. It seems Ernest has run off. No one can find him."

ERNEST GOES DOWN HARD

Ernest had made it to North Side Park just as his adrenaline ran out. It was probably a good thing, because fatigue stopped him from running into the woods frantically and getting himself lost. Forced to slow down and catch his breath, he gave his mind a chance to pause and actually take in his surroundings.

It was dark out, but not so dark that Ernest couldn't find the right trail to lead him to the cave. The rain was coming down harder, though, and he was really looking forward to getting that windbreaker.

He started climbing up the slope to the cave entrance, but the rain had made the ground muddy and slick. The farther he got up the slope, the more he kept sliding back. Ernest remembered an old Greek story about a guy who had to keep rolling a boulder up a hill, only to have it roll back down to the bottom every time. That was how Ernest felt now, only he was the boulder.

Ryan had been right about him. Right about all of it. He was just a sheltered little kid who thought he could fix everything, but in the end only made it worse. What hurt most of all wasn't that Ryan had been right, but that Grandpa Eddie had been wrong. Wrong about Ernest, wrong to entrust him with his last, dying wish.

Ernest was now on all fours climbing up the slope. He could see the cave opening just a few feet in front of him, only no matter how hard he dug and clawed at the loose earth beneath him, he couldn't close that last little distance. But he wouldn't stop trying. He'd keep at it all night if he had to.

And he would have, too, if the ground beneath him hadn't completely given way.

It was like having a rug pulled out from under him. Ernest face-planted into the mud, and the next thing he knew he was rolling down the hill, along with half the slope. The mudslide was sudden and fierce and so powerful that he was too shocked to even be scared.

On instinct, Ernest reached out for something to grab on to. He grasped at anything that would keep him from falling, and finally his arm wrapped around the trunk of a tree about twenty yards from the trail.

And then his luck got worse.

His arm snapped, just above the elbow.

22

AFRAID

It was only a matter of time before the factory would close. Ryan's mom told them that Mr. Wilmette didn't get the bank loan before they ended their call. But Ryan couldn't think about that now. Ernest was missing.

After Mr. Earle hung up the phone, Ryan told him that they had to go to North Side Park. He was sure that Ernest was going back to the cave, back to the beginning. The poor kid probably thought a wish of his own might make everything okay. Tess grabbed some flashlights and then called the fire department from her cell phone as Mr. Earle drove them hurriedly to the park.

"Ernest!" Ryan called, running down the paths, his flashlight panning the woods frantically. "Ernest!"

"You're too far ahead!" Mr. Earle called, but Ryan sprinted deeper into the woods. There was no sign of Ernest. Ryan was having a harder time than expected navigating the trails in the dark and the rain. The search was starting to look hopeless.

Ryan was scared now. He had a strong feeling that this was one of those fateful moments, the kind where things could go either way.

Then an unwelcome thought flashed in Ryan's mind as quickly and as forcefully as he tried to push it out.

Rollo. This whole thing had started sixty years ago because a sweet kid with a big heart died. What if that's how this story ends, too?

"Ryan!" he heard Mr. Earle yell again, from farther away.

Ryan started running helter-skelter, calling out to Ernest in a voice that was increasingly loud and increasingly desperate. But it wasn't working. He ran faster, shouted until he was hoarse. The trees began to all look the same; the paths twisted and spun until they were unrecognizable.

And then he stopped. He didn't know where he was any longer, and he couldn't hear Mr. Earle and Tess calling to him.

Ryan was starting to panic. He could feel fear getting the better of him, just as it had the other night when Lizzy had told them about Andrea Chase. When he'd said those awful things to Ernest. He wasn't going to let fear take over again.

Ryan closed his eyes and slowed down his breathing. He was still scared. Terrified, actually. But he realized that it didn't matter if he was afraid. What mattered was putting the fear in its place.

Ryan opened his eyes and slowly scanned the woods with his flashlight. He was at an intersection between two trails. The beam of light landed on a wooden trail marker. Good. *Mile 0.5* was etched into the wood and painted blue.

He knew this marker. He'd overshot the cave.

Ryan doubled back on the trail. He was getting his bearings; the trail was feeling more familiar, even in the dark. He picked his pace up to a steady jog. He could hear Mr. Earle and Tess now, but they still sounded far away.

He didn't answer. He was thinking.

Ryan found the spot where they would always leave the trail and hike the woods to the cave. He stepped off the trail, slowly now, and shined his flashlight. He started calling for Ernest, but was more intent on listening.

Just then, a flash of lightning lit up the woods all around him. For a brief moment everything went suddenly, deathly quiet.

Less than a second later the woods were plunged into darkness again, but the flash had been long enough for Ryan to see what he needed to see.

A LATE-NIGHT RUN

It was a slow night in the firehouse. Chad Finnegan was stacking the CPR dummies in the supply room when Chief Collins poked his head in the door.

"Finnegan?"

"Hey, Chief."

"Some kid wandered into the Nature Preserve off North Side Park. You run those trails, don't you?"

"Yes, sir."

"Suit up. You're with Jenkins and Rafferty. Two minutes."

BROKEN BONES AND MUD SKIING

Ryan hurried to the spot on the hill where he'd seen, in that brief, illuminated moment, a prone figure lying in the mud. It was Ernest, facedown, half-conscious and moaning softly, his left arm bent at an impossible angle.

Ryan crouched. "Ernest," he said. "Can you hear me?"

Ernest moaned in pain. The storm raged overhead, the lightning and thunder coming back-to-back as the rain came down fast and hard. Ryan heard a rumbling sound. At first he thought it was more thunder. But then he felt it.

Beneath him.

"We need to get you out of here." Ryan struggled to lift Ernest without upsetting his broken arm, but it wasn't easy. Every twitch and shift caused Ernest to gasp from the pain, and Ryan feared that if he moved him too quickly, his friend might go into shock.

But that rumbling was getting stronger.

Ryan took a deep breath and then hooked his head under Ernest's good arm. Ryan got him up halfway and Ernest promptly vomited. With uncertain legs on uncertain earth, Ryan summoned all his strength and hoisted Ernest up in a fireman's carry.

Then, with small, hurried steps, he made his way down the slope.

Ryan felt the ground sliding underneath him. It was kind of like skiing, but without skis. Behind him, he heard a great crashing sound, and even though he didn't dare look back, he knew what it was.

The entire hill was collapsing on itself.

Ryan decided his best bet was to ride the mudslide. He could see the bottom of the hill and the trail a few yards beyond, and braced himself for the worst. He knew that when they reached the bottom, the mud would stop sliding abruptly and he'd have to be ready.

Sure enough, the slope leveled out and the ground beneath him settled, and he felt like he was being shoved forward. Ryan managed two, three long strides before inertia overtook him and he began to pitch forward onto the trail.

We're going down hard, Ryan thought.

But as fate or chance or destiny or magic would have it, Mr. Earle was there to catch them.

Though *catch* might be an overstatement. Mr. Earle did slow their bodies with his own, so that when they all fell to the ground, the kids landed on him, which probably prevented a concussion or two. But Ryan twisted his right ankle badly, and the collision made Ernest cry out and faint from the pain.

Mr. Earle, who suffered a broken nose courtesy of Ryan's forehead, managed to scoop up Ernest in his arms. Ryan couldn't put any pressure at all on his right leg, but then Tess, who had been searching another trail, found them. She went directly for Ryan, hooking his arm around her neck and guiding him and the others out of the woods toward a large oak tree in the middle of the park. She rested Ryan gently against the massive trunk and then helped Mr. Earle lay Ernest out and elevate his legs. Tess then took off her jacket and covered Ernest's chest with it while Mr. Earle inspected him for more injuries.

It was an old oak tree with a thick canopy of leaves that kept out much of the rain. The storm was finally passing, it seemed. While they were tending to Ernest, Mr. Earle shot Ryan a concerned look. Ryan gave his teacher a short nod. Ernest needed the help more.

Then Ryan closed his eyes. His leg was throbbing, he was soaked to the bone, and there was a cold bite to the wind, but he didn't care. Because Ernest was alive. His friend was alive and right now that was everything.

His eyes popped open at the sound of lightning striking a nearby maple tree. Right in front of him, along the tree line of the Nature Preserve, he saw the maple split cleanly down the middle and fall majestically toward the ground.

Completely smashing Thompkins Well.

WHERE IN CLIFFS DONNELLY IS ERNEST WILMETTE'S WINDBREAKER?

"Ryan?"

"What?"

"Are you up?"

Ryan opened his eyes and looked over at Ernest. They were

both lying on stretchers in the back of an ambulance. An EMT sat on a little bench between them. "I guess so."

"We have a problem," Ernest said.

"We're in the back of an ambulance, Ernest. That pretty much goes without saying."

"No, not that," Ernest said. "My windbreaker."

"What?"

"I left it in the cave. What if someone finds it?"

Ryan thought for a moment. "You're telling me that's why you went into the woods tonight? To get your windbreaker out of the cave?"

"Uh-huh," Ernest said.

Ryan started to giggle.

"Ryan?"

But Ryan was laughing harder now, the kind of laughter that takes over everything and makes your whole body shake. Which, considering Ryan's current state, actually hurt more than a little.

"I'm sorry, Ryan. I tried. I really tried."

The desperation in Ernest's voice sobered Ryan up just enough to regain himself.

"Ernest," Ryan said. "Your windbreaker isn't in the cave. It's at my house. You left it there when you slept over last month."

BOYS

Chad leaned back against the cab as the ambulance sped toward the hospital.

"ETA seven minutes," Rafferty said through the cab window. "How are they doing?"

Chad glanced down at the two boys on either side of him. "Good," Chad said. "Quiet."

The bigger of the two boys looked to be about twelve, the other one younger. Or maybe just smaller.

The little one started talking to the bigger one. He had scared eyes, not that you could blame him. That was a nasty break.

Chad remembered when he had broken his leg. He was thirteen. He and Matt Redigger had gone jumping off Pike Road Bridge into Fulton Creek.

He had been scared, too. Like the little one here with the broken arm, looking to his friend to tell him it would be all right.

That's what Matt had done for him. Made it all right.

The two boys were whispering across their stretchers now. Then the bigger one started laughing.

"Okay back there?" Rafferty asked from the cab.

Chad wasn't sure. The bigger one might be going into shock. But then the little one started to laugh, too.

"Yeah," Chad said. "They're okay."

BUDDY THE FORGOTTEN

They were half a mile away from the house when Lizzy's mom groaned in that way people do when they remember something truly inconvenient.

"What?" Lizzy said as her mom did a U-turn in the middle of the street.

"We have to go back to the hospital." Her mom sighed.

"Okay. What did you forget?"

"Not what," her mom said wearily. "Who."

SNAP, CRACKLE, POP

Ernest's mom and Mrs. Hardy met the ambulance as it pulled up to the hospital. Ernest knew he should be scared to see his mother. He'd be in big trouble for running off, getting lost in the woods, and breaking his arm. But what Ryan had told him about his windbreaker made him so happy he just couldn't worry about anything else.

It was a compound fracture. The doctor gave Ernest a shot before setting it, to dull the pain. The medicine worked fast. The last thing he remembered was two nurses holding him down, one by the shoulders, one by the legs, while the doctor grabbed his arm below the elbow and counted down from three. At *one* Ernest heard a pop, followed by several loud crackling sounds.

Shouldn't that hurt? Ernest thought.

And then he was out.

OVERTIME

"How long has he been in there?"

"Since about five thirty," Jeanne said.

"What? That's over three hours!"

"I told him he could go at seven," Jeanne said. "He wanted to stay."

Julia MacComber looked through the window into the neonatal ICU. Buddy was sitting beside the unit's one patient, singing softly into the little incubator.

"Well, that's a surprise," she said. Then she headed for the elevators. Lizzy would be waiting.

PATCHING UP

Lizzy was indeed waiting for her mom by the ER admitting desk when Ryan hobbled out of a nearby exam room.

A nurse had put a brace on Ryan's ankle, cleaned and bandaged his head, and taped up his ribs.

Ryan gave Lizzy a quick rundown on the last few hours—Andrea Chase arrested, Ernest upstairs with a broken arm, secrets safe, cave completely covered in landslide, and Thompkins Well destroyed—and promised a fuller account in good time.

"Where's your mom?" Lizzy asked.

"Outside, trying to reach my dad on his cell."

Lizzy rushed off to find her own mother just as Ryan's dad and Mr. Wilmette arrived at the hospital. They had been at the factory, which got spotty cell reception even in good weather and virtually none in a storm like this. As such they hadn't gotten any of their wives' frantic messages over the last hour until about fifteen minutes ago.

Ryan stood up as the two men converged on him.

"Ernest?" Mr. Wilmette said, his voice sounding small, timid even.

"Broken arm. No concussion. He's sleeping, Room 314."

Mr. Wilmette hurried off to find his son. Ryan's dad took in his own.

"You look terrible," Doug Hardy said, a strained smile on his face and a whole lot of fear in his eyes.

"I'm okay," Ryan said. "I heard about the loan."

"Never mind the loan," his dad said, trembling as he wrapped his arms around Ryan and pulled him closer. Ryan could feel the man's frame shaking as he held his son, afraid to let go.

For the first time in months, Ryan was not afraid.

But he didn't let go, either.

23

A SERIOUS TALK

Ernest's parents sat on the edge of his hospital bed and looked at him. They'd been doing that all day, like they were afraid they might lose him if they looked away.

His dad said that they were very sorry about keeping Ernest in the dark these last few months and that they should have talked to him about what was going on with the factory and the bank. This statement took Ernest by surprise, because it was not immediately followed by the word *but*. Ernest's parents said they were sorry, with no qualifications.

His dad even promised to fix the problem. He and Ernest's

mom were going to be more honest and open with Ernest about things that affected them all as a family.

Starting now.

"Three months ago," said his dad, "the factory won a big contract with an international corporation that's opening up a new plant in Cincinnati."

It was great news, wonderful news. Not just for Ernest and his family. But for the factory. For the town.

The only problem was that, to guarantee enough product to secure the contract, his dad would need to expand the factory.

"But isn't that a good thing?" Ernest asked.

"A very good thing," his dad replied. "Expanding means I can hire more people. The problem is that expanding costs money."

"So that's why you were putting Grandpa Eddie's house on the market," Ernest said to his mom.

She nodded. "Except your grandfather's house is very old, and on that side of town . . ." His mom stopped short. "Well, let's just say we wouldn't get enough on the sale to make a difference one way or the other."

"The bank just won't play ball, Ernest," his dad said.

Suddenly, Ernest could understand why his parents had been so stressed and distant. It's bad enough having a problem. But to create a solution and then have someone stop you from making it work—that could drive a person nuts.

"So, Ernest," his dad said, looking squarely at his son. "What do you think?"

Ernest thought he understood everything his parents had told him. But then he figured he must have missed something, because the answer seemed so simple, so obvious.

"Why not sell our house?" Ernest said. "It's worth a lot more, right?"

"Well, yes," his mom said. "But where will we live?"

"Grandpa Eddie's house."

His dad and his mom looked at each other.

"I think it's a great idea, son," his dad said.

Hope and doubt were fighting it out across his mother's face. "Will it be enough?"

His dad shrugged. "I don't know. But it's worth a shot."

RUMMAGE SALE

Old shirts. Old dresses. So many old-people clothes.

This was not how Jeanne had planned to spend her day off. Sorting through old clothes. She'd just come off a double shift at the hospital where she was a nurse in the neonatal unit, and she was exhausted. But her mom gave her that whole "you work all the time and I never get to see you anymore" guilt trip, and so here they were, down in the church basement, tagging old junk for the bi-monthly rummage sale.

The boxes on Jeanne's table were donated by the grand-daughter of an old parishioner who had recently died. Jeanne had been sorting through boxes for the better part of an hour, and there were still three or four boxes left.

She grabbed the next one, which was filled with random items: a toaster, some garden shears, a wall clock, and a . . . What the . . .

In the bottom of the pile was a really old box, still in good shape. She pulled it out of the pile for a closer look.

It was a ray gun. A really old toy ray gun. Like from the fifties. Never been opened.

A Flash Gordon click ray pistol, according to the box. Jeanne had no earthly clue what most of that meant, but enough of her boyfriend Drew's geek-speak had filtered into her brain to rec-ognize the name Flash Gordon. The box itself was sci-fi gold. It was decorated with a drawing of Flash Gordon with what looked like a five-gallon water-cooler bottle on his head, shooting his laser pistol at some creepy goblin-like alien.

She carefully opened the box to check inside. The pistol was in perfect condition.

Drew would go nuts for this.

THE REDIGGERS

Chad Finnegan had been sitting in his car for about ten minutes, parked half a block down from the house. He'd driven by this house a lot since he first got home, sometimes three or four times a week. Wanting to stop but too afraid to go through with it.

But something about those two boys in the back of the ambulance last night—the little one with the broken arm, the bigger one with the crazy laugh—told him it was time.

SETTLING ACCOUNTS

Ryan spent the next day on the couch, his ankle propped on a pillow, watching movies with his dad. Lizzy came over after school. She was still pretty keyed up over the last couple of days and couldn't decide whether to hug him or punch him in the arm as hard as she could. So she did both.

And in both cases, Ryan just took it.

Then, late in the afternoon, Ryan had some other visitors. Mr. Earle came over with Tess. The light of day wasn't doing any favors to the beating Mr. Earle had taken on last night's little adventure. If anything, he looked worse. His face had swollen and bruised overnight and he had two black eyes along with the broken nose courtesy of Ryan's forehead.

Tess, by contrast, was completely put together. She wore a gray suit with heels and carried a leather briefcase. And she was acting a little different, too. Kind of serious, professional even, like she was here on business.

Which, it turned out, she was.

She took a seat across from Ryan and his parents. "Remember last night, when I told you that my grandmother wasn't senile, that she knew you weren't letting her pay you?" she said. "Well, this is what she did with that money."

She removed a small stack of documents from her briefcase and handed Ryan the top page. It was a quarterly earnings report for an investment portfolio made out in his name.

"I don't understand," Ryan said.

"Since you were too kind to ever take her money," Tess explained, "she started putting money aside for you, in a trust. She then invested that money in a start-up I was financing." She pointed to a highlighted number at the bottom of the page. "You could say that it took off."

Ryan looked at the highlighted number, the portfolio's net worth. It was a really big number. The kind of number people from the South Side don't come across that often.

"Holy . . . wow," his dad said.

"It's not enough to buy a house on the Riviera," Tess said. "But it should help out with college."

Ryan looked at his mom. "Looks like you're going back to school," he said.

"What?" his mom said, stunned. "No, honey. That's for you—"

"And I'm investing it," Ryan said. He gave his dad a look. "My business, right?"

"It certainly is," his dad said.

JOSH GETS HIS WISH

Josh Redigger came home to the sound of laughing in the kitchen.

It had already been a weird day at school. Ernest Wilmette and Ryan Hardy were both absent, and there was a sub in Mr. Earle's class. A lot of rumors were circulating through the school about an incident in the woods last night. The most popular of these had Mr. Earle rescuing Ernest and Ryan from a devil-worshipping cult sacrifice.

"In here, Josh!" his mom called to him from the kitchen. He dropped his bag and went in. There he saw his mom and dad sitting at the kitchen table with . . .

"Chad!"

"Hey, buddy," Chad said, getting up and giving Josh a bear hug. "You've gotten taller."

"Eh, barely," Josh said as he sat down at the table.

"Chad and your father were just reminiscing about the time he taught the boys how to drive a stick shift."

"Your brother," Chad said to Josh, "kept looking down whenever he had to shift."

"And drifting across the center line," his dad added.

"So then your dad yells, 'Matt! Eyes on the road!' and Matt panics, looks up, and yanks his foot off the clutch."

Josh's father laughed. "That poor car never drove the same after you two boys."

Chad and his parents went on like this for hours. Josh had no idea what in the heck they were talking about. But he didn't care. He just didn't want them to stop.

HAPPINESS IS A WARM FLASH GORDON CLICK RAY PISTOL

"Are you *sure*?" the woman asked, brushing her hand lightly on top of the airline agent's. "I know there are first-class seats available. I checked online."

She was pretty, strikingly so. Pretty enough to be on TV.

Drew had seen plenty of her kind before. The kind used to getting her way.

"I'm sorry, Ms. Chase," he said. "But we're not offering any upgrades for this flight."

The woman huffed indignantly and walked away.

Drew took out his phone and looked at the text again. It was from his girlfriend, Jeanne. She had sent him a photo attachment, a picture of . . . He still couldn't believe it.

An original Louis Marx Flash Gordon click ray pistol. Mint condition!

It was an awesome find, to be sure. But the best part, the very best part, was that Jeanne found it. He knew she secretly hated that stuff (well, not secretly, though patiently, at least). But she got it for him anyway.

Drew looked up and saw a lady with kind yet tired eyes standing quietly at his station.

"Oh, I'm sorry," he said, embarrassed. "Um, checking in?"

"No worries." The lady smiled and handed Drew her ticket.

The reservation appeared on the screen. *Evelyn Reeves.* She'd booked two days ago.

Drew looked back up at the lady. Working the service desk, you get pretty good at reading faces. Evelyn Reeves, Drew knew, was not traveling for fun. The recently booked ticket, the sad patience in her eyes. She was either going to a funeral or to see a very sick relative.

Drew worked his computer. "Going to New York, then continuing on to Boston?"

"Yes, sir," Evelyn Reeves said softly.

Drew hit a few more keys and printed up her boarding passes. "Here you go, Mrs. Reeves," he said. He leaned forward furtively as he handed her the passes. "I hope you don't mind," he whispered, "but I upgraded you to first class for both legs."

Mrs. Reeves took the passes, confused. "I . . . Thank you," she said, emitting the tiniest breath of surprise. "Thank you so much."

Drew smiled. "Have a good flight, Mrs. Reeves."

24

OLD HOUSE, NEW BEGINNING

"Ernest!" his mom called from downstairs.

"Coming, Mom."

On his way from his bedroom, Ernest had to pass the steps leading up to that creepy attic door. It didn't scare him anymore, though. Summer vacation had just begun, and this had been his house for a while now.

It was the first of many welcome changes for Ernest Wilmette. There was a time, shortly after Ernest had come home from the hospital in a massive cast that ran the length of his arm, when he feared his parents would treat him like a fragile little baby doll for the rest of his life. But to his surprise, Ernest's injury actually toughened him up in his parents' eyes.

For starters, his parents let him ride in the front seat, following a late fall growth spurt. (Well, more of a growth trickle, to be accurate.) Ernest's dad had even promised to teach him how to mow the lawn this summer.

And they talked to him more, told him more, about both big and small things. In fact, one day while looking through some ancient family photos, Ernest's dad pointed out an eccentric old lady, Great-Aunt Myrtle. Obsessed with catastrophe, she notoriously gave out the worst birthday and Christmas presents—a first aid kit, a canteen, water purification tablets, maybe a ham radio, or, on special occasions . . .

. . . a fire extinguisher.

Because, as Great-Aunt Myrtle was often fond of saying, *you never know.*

When Ernest got downstairs, Declan was already in his chair eating apple slices.

"Was Ryan here?" Ernest asked.

"Just to drop off Declan," his mom said. "He has to do the Haemmerle lawn this morning."

Ryan's mom had started going back to school three days a week at Ohio State, and Ernest's mom looked after Declan on the days when Mrs. Hardy was at class or studying.

In fact, over the last few months the Wilmette house had become an unofficial after-school hub for Ernest and his friends. Ryan and Lizzy were over most afternoons, and sometimes Lizzy brought along her cousin Amber. Tommy and Winston stopped by now and again. The house was often loud and busy, and there was always someone tracking in dirt, making a mess, adding to the chaos.

Ernest knew that's how his mom liked it. Crowded, loud, messy. Home.

"Dad already gone?"

"He and Mr. Hardy were out the door first thing," his mom said. Ryan's dad was in charge of the expansion and had become Ernest's dad's second-in-command at the factory.

As Ernest had suggested, his dad had put their house on the market last fall, just before Thanksgiving. It sold quickly to a very motivated buyer, and Ernest and his family moved into Grandpa Eddie's old house.

Even though Ernest's dad got a great price for the house, the money still fell far short of covering the proposed expansion. But once word had gotten out that the Wilmette family was putting up their own money, their own house, even, to save the factory and, to no small degree, the town, people responded.

People like Marcus Earle and Tess Haemmerle. Like Detective Stanley Donan (Ret.) and Jack Hought. Dr. Tom Shay and Dr. Salman Patil. Lizzy's mom and the nurses she worked with, along with the doctors, orderlies, and administrators. And lots of other people Ernest didn't even know.

People who had wishes.

Or people who just had hope.

And all those people, well, they weren't shy about letting one R. Peter Bilkes, the president of Donnelly Fidelity Bank, know that they were considering pulling their money from his bank. R. Peter Bilkes, a great believer in the almighty bottom line, decided it was maybe time to recheck some of his figures.

Wilmette Stamping, Tool & Die got the loan just in time for Christmas.

KEEPING IT IN THE FAMILY

After dropping off Declan at the Wilmettes' house, Ryan went across the street to Mrs. Haemmerle's old house. Ever since the funeral, Tess had been splitting her time between Cliffs Donnelly and San Francisco. Ryan was surprised when she didn't put her grandmother's house on the market, then less surprised when Tess and Mr. Earle started seeing each other.

Tess waved at Ryan from the kitchen window as he walked up to the garage. He waved back. When Tess was in California, she left Ryan in charge of looking after the house. That meant his usual yard work, but also taking in the mail and generally keeping an eye on the place. She paid him, of course, but in truth he would have been happy to do it for free.

Ryan opened the garage and topped off the lawn mower with gas. As he put the gas can back, he recalled the time, last fall, when Ernest had come over with a bag containing Rollo's remaining birthday gifts, a quilt and a toy ray gun. He'd used the quilt when Mrs. Haemmerle died, but to this day he had no idea what ever happened to that ray gun. Sometimes he thought he might find it buried behind some old boxes in the garage, but deep down he knew it was gone.

FRIENDS LIKE THESE

"You look lovely."

"I look ridiculous."

"Stop that," Lizzy's mother said. They had just gotten Lizzy's bridesmaid dress back from the tailor, and her mom couldn't wait to make her try it on.

Lizzy's mom and Dr. Shay were getting married in the fall. It was going to be a small wedding, just family and a few close friends. Dr. Shay's brother was the best man and Lizzy was her mom's maid of honor, but that was it for the bridal party.

"I need to get a picture to send Tom," she said, taking out her phone.

"Mom," Lizzy groaned.

"Ugh. The light in here is terrible," her mom said, trying different angles for the picture. "Let's go outside."

"Mom!" Lizzy groaned with heightened emphasis.

It was no use. Lizzy's mom would not be deterred. She put down the phone, took Lizzy's hand in both of hers, and led her outside.

Then she remembered the phone.

"Stay there," she said. "Be right back."

Lizzy stood on the front lawn, hoping no one would come down the street for the next three to five minutes.

"Hey," Ryan said as he dragged Mrs. Haemmerle's trash bins up from the curb. "A little early for back-to-school shopping, isn't it?"

"Shut up," Lizzy snapped. "It's my dress for the wedding."

"I figured," Ryan said.

Lizzy fidgeted when he didn't say anything after that.

"You don't like it," she said.

"I do," he insisted.

"It's okay. You don't have to pretend."

"I'm not pretending," he said.

"I just know that, well, dresses aren't really my thing."

"Lizzy," Ryan said, "I've already told you once I thought you were pretty."

"That time didn't count."

"Yes, it did."

"Nope," she said. "I was crying. You felt compelled."

"I meant it."

"Still doesn't count." She wasn't going to budge.

"I meant it," he said directly. "I *mean* it. You are pretty. Really pretty. And not just because of all this," he said, waving his hands to suggest the dress, her hair, face, and everything else. "Lizzy, you are pretty all the way through."

She hadn't expected that, and it made her gasp a little. The best part, though, was that while it was certainly nice to hear, she was surprised to discover it wasn't something she *needed* to hear.

Even from Ryan Hardy.

And that, Lizzy realized, was perhaps what she had really wanted all along.

After her mom finally finished taking pictures of her in her bridesmaid dress, Lizzy changed as fast as she could back into her regular clothes, had a quick sandwich for lunch, and then went to get Ernest.

About two weeks before the end of the school year, Mr. Earle's old Sunday school teacher, a woman named Evelyn Reeves, had asked him for a favor. She had sold a kids' book to a big New York publishing house and was about to turn in her final manuscript to her editor. First, however, she wondered if Mr. Earle had any students he thought might be up for taking her novel out for a test drive.

Naturally, he thought of Ernest and Lizzy.

The book was called *Friends Like These*. It was about a thirteen-year-old boy named Stuart in a small New England town who discovers one day that his best friend, Nash, is secretly, and literally, a devil. It was scary and dangerous, of course, with lots of demons and angels (who can be surprisingly scarier than the demons) and angry mobs of frightened townspeople (who can be, less surprisingly to Lizzy, scarier than both), but Stuart sticks by his friend. Because that's what you do, even if your friend comes from the wrong side of the tracks.

Lizzy loved the book and had even tried to get Ryan to read it, but with no success. Now she and Ernest were meeting Mrs. Reeves and Mr. Earle at the school to discuss it and give her feedback before she sent the final revision to her publisher.

As Lizzy approached Ernest's house, a thick, manila envelope tucked under her arm, she couldn't help but think about her cousin Chelsea. It was Chelsea's parents who had bought Ernest's house on the North Side. Once Lizzy's mom made it abundantly clear that neither she nor Lizzy would be apologizing to Chelsea or Aunt Patty, Lizzy's uncle Ron had to do something to appease his domineering wife and daughter.

Fortunately for him, the most coveted house in town was about to be put on the market.

Funny how things work out like that.

And while it might have irked Lizzy that Chelsea and Aunt Patty had been, in a way, rewarded for their many acts of petty, and not so petty, cruelty, she tried not to dwell on it.

Besides, the move was a godsend to poor Amber. While Aunt Patty was absorbed with the new house, and Chelsea was absorbed with, well, Chelsea, Amber could now devote the energy she'd previously spent on hiding in plain sight on more rewarding pursuits. Like sports (she was quite the volleyball player), and hanging out with Lizzy. Lizzy had never forgotten the way Amber had silently sat beside her that day when she had finally stood up to Chelsea. It was a little thing, perhaps.

But the strongest friendships are often based on the little things.

When Lizzy got to the house, Ernest was waiting eagerly on the front steps.

"What's that?" he asked, pointing at the envelope as he hopped off the steps.

"The manuscript," Lizzy said. "I took some notes."

"Like, active reading notes?" Ernest said, suddenly worried. "Were we supposed to do that? Because I didn't do that."

"I'm sure it's fine."

"I mean, I just read it," he went on, "like for fun, you know?"

He was getting worked up. Ernest's ability to overthink things amazed Lizzy sometimes. You'd think after everything they'd been through together, he'd have figured out how not to sweat the small stuff.

"Ernest . . ." Lizzy said slowly.

"I could go back inside and get—"

"Ernest," she said, less slowly.

He stopped, looking at her searchingly. "Relax?"

"Relax," Lizzy said.

"Okay."

THE ONE THAT GOT AWAY

Ryan was sitting at Mrs. Haemmerle's kitchen table with Tess when Ernest and Lizzy came to the door. He still thought of it as Mrs. Haemmerle's kitchen; he suspected Tess did, too. If she was in town when he did the lawn, she always invited him in for a sandwich, or a drink and a cookie. Sometimes they'd talk; sometimes they'd just sit in the kitchen together, and that was nice, too.

"We're heading over to school now," Ernest said. "Want to come?"

"I don't know," Ryan said, doubtfully. "I didn't read the book."

"That's okay. Mr. Earle didn't get to read it, either."

Ryan didn't really feel like it, but Tess caught his eye and she gave him a look that said, *Go live, have fun, be young.*

"Yeah, okay," he said.

As they walked to school, Ernest and Lizzy were going back and forth about the book, talking a mile a minute, and Ryan felt himself tagging along a bit behind them.

He didn't mind.

Ryan had done his best in the last several months to avoid thinking too much about everything that had happened in the past year. And though it had all worked out better than he'd ever dared hope, sometimes he still felt . . . cheated.

It was ridiculous, he knew. He was lucky he wasn't in juvie for attempted burglary. He had no right to complain. Still, there was one wish that he'd really wanted to come true, one really important time the well came up short, and it nagged at him.

THE NEW THOMPKINS WELL

Mr. Earle had propped open the front door for them. As they entered the school, Ernest noticed Ryan drifting over toward the courtyard.

Last April, while Rod Serling Middle School had been closed for spring break, Winston Patil and Tommy Bricks had completely covered the courtyard in tarps to shield their work from any outside view.

Then, six weeks later, on the Friday before Memorial Day weekend, the tarps came down, and their secret project was finally revealed. In the center of the courtyard, Tommy had carefully constructed a full-sized replica of Thompkins Well out of junk. The entire structure was made up of various pieces of discarded scrap and detritus, broken, twisted fragments of metal and plastic and wood and brick—all this refuse that had once been pieces of other things, but was now put back together in a different way to make something new.

Something special.

Then, on that ugly cinder-block back wall, the one that was supposed to have been glass instead of the concrete eyesore it had been for decades, Winston had painted a massive two-story mural of the town of Cliffs Donnelly, drawn meticulously to scale and with all the local landmarks represented in painstaking detail.

The courtyard was unveiled to minimal fanfare. There'd been a brief assembly at the beginning of the school day, a dedication and polite applause, and that had been that.

No reporters. No television cameras.

It did not trend on social media.

But then, as the weeks passed, people started adding their own little touches to the courtyard. A laminated page on convergence insufficiency from an old medical textbook appeared inside the well. It was joined by a pair of old running shoes, slightly singed on the sides and still smelling of burnt leaves. A few days after that, a tiny ID bracelet from the infant care ward showed up. Then a first pay stub from Wilmette Stamping, Tool & Die. And so on.

It wasn't something anyone expected, but sometimes things just take on a life of their own. Tommy's replica of Thompkins Well had originally been conceived simply as a statue to honor the beloved local landmark. But since the actual Thompkins Well had been destroyed last fall (maple tree, lightning), the people of Cliffs Donnelly began to adopt Tommy's replica as a kind of replacement for the obliterated original. A Thompkins Well 2.0. Before long, the new Thompkins Well became a local landmark in its own right. A place where people could go to hope, to wish, and to create their own stories.

Ernest and Lizzy turned down the hall toward Mr. Earle's room. Ryan was still lagging behind, staring into the courtyard.

"You guys go ahead," he said. "I'll catch up later."

THE WELL'S LAST LAUGH

"They did a heck of a job, didn't they?"

Ryan turned to find Mr. Earle standing by the windows next to him. "Yeah," he said. "They really did. So, it must have been a pretty big surprise to hear that your old Sunday school teacher is about to be a famous author?"

"Nah, not really," Mr. Earle said. "She was always good at telling stories."

"Yeah?"

"Oh, yeah," Mr. Earle said, then smiled just a little. "Where do you think I learned it?"

They were quiet for a moment. Then Ryan said, "I have to know—do you believe any of it? The well, the wishes, Ernest's attic full of old toys?"

Mr. Earle looked at him quizzically. "Do you mean, do I believe *you*?"

"Well, yeah."

"I believe you told me the truth."

"That's only half an answer," Ryan said. "I'm asking—"

"If I believe in miracles?"

Ryan gave him a look that said, *You said it, I didn't, but since you said it, do you?*

Mr. Earle shifted his weight from one foot to the other as he thought about it. "Do you remember when I first told the class the story of Thompkins Well?"

"Yeah. During Council."

"And we talked about folklore and legends and the reasons we have for telling the stories we tell?"

Ryan nodded.

"And you said fear. To teach kids to be afraid and obedient."

"I thought that kind of cheesed you off, when I said that."

Mr. Earle shook his head. "No, you were right. But there's another reason, one nobody mentioned that day. Stories bind us together; they connect us. Our stories are a shared history, a way to relate to each other. Even if they are make-believe." Mr. Earle shrugged his shoulders. "I don't know if Thompkins Well could grant wishes or not. And I really don't care. I do know that you and your friends helped a lot of people. For me, that's all that matters."

Ryan and Mr. Earle returned to the classroom just as Ernest, Lizzy, and Mrs. Reeves finished talking about the book. Mrs. Reeves had brought homemade cookies and lemonade, and she told them stories about what Mr. Earle was like as a kid.

Then Ernest asked her how she got her book published, and she started to tell a curious story.

She said that she had begun writing the book during a difficult time for her family. Her husband had just sustained a work injury that cost him a good job. Money was tight, and they were worried they would lose their house. To top it all off, her own mother was very sick, dying actually, in Boston, but they didn't think they could afford to send her there in time to say goodbye.

What she didn't know was that her son had been secretly putting money aside from his part-time job at the grocery store to pay for her plane ticket. Mrs. Reeves told them about how he'd come into the kitchen, a handful of crumpled bills in his hand.

It was at this point that Ryan started to get a funny feeling running up the back of his neck.

Pressed by her family to make the trip to Boston, Mrs. Reeves had bought a last-minute ticket with her son's money. By some quirk of fate and generosity, Mrs. Reeves was bumped up to first class, where she sat next to a book editor for a major New York publishing house.

Ryan sat motionless in his seat, an unnerving but not unpleasant chill running through his entire body.

"You okay?" Lizzy whispered, nudging Ryan lightly in his side.

"Huh?" he said, turning to her.

"You look like you saw a ghost or something."

Ryan said, "No, I'm good." And left it at that.

It was late in the afternoon when Mrs. Reeves's husband pulled up in front of the school. She thanked Lizzy and Ernest for their help, hugging them warmly.

"And thank you, Marcus," Mrs. Reeves said, kissing him lightly on the cheek.

"Anytime, Mrs. Reeves," Mr. Earle said, and for a minute Ryan thought he could see what his teacher had been like as a kid.

As Mrs. Reeves approached the car, Ryan watched a boy a couple of years older than him get out of the passenger's seat and climb into the back to give his mom the front seat. The boy happened to look Ryan's way for just a second and they locked eyes.

Ryan knew.

He was the boy at the well. The one whose story had hit Ryan the hardest of them all. The wish that got away.

And Ryan didn't even care that he'd never have any idea how it had all worked out in the end. How a toy ray gun that was meant for Rollo Wilmette—the only gift left—had gotten from Mrs. Haemmerle's garage to wherever it needed to go to make sure Evelyn Reeves was seated next to a book publisher. In fact, not knowing made it better.

Because Ryan realized that for every wish he knew about, there must have been dozens that he didn't. Maybe that was the point, in the end. You can't fix the world. But you do your best in your own little corner of it.

And you hope.

INTO THE DARK

Tommy couldn't remember ever really being afraid of the dark. From an early age, he always had more practical things to fear.

But tonight was really dark. There was no moon out and the sky was pitch-black. The houses on this block weren't big on porch lights, either, so it was hard to see the road in front of him.

It was spooky quiet, too.

They'd set out around three in the morning, riding their bikes across the sleeping town. Tommy carried a duffel bag, the straps looped around his arms like a backpack. The bulky contents slammed into his spine as he pedaled. He hadn't expected Winston to come along and was still surprised that he'd wanted to. When Tommy first told him what he planned to do, shortly after the unveiling of the new Thompkins Well, he made sure to say it so Winston knew he wasn't on the hook, that it was okay if he wasn't comfortable with the idea.

But Winston was in, right from the start. Tommy realized he

should have expected as much. Ever since that night in the storm, Winston had become someone Tommy could always count on. Tommy knew he was never completely alone.

But he also knew that there was a big difference between *better* and *all better*. Because while over the last several months the Patil house had become a second home for Tommy, it was still just a *second* home. And he still had years left to live in his first. Tommy knew those years would have their share of his father's drunken rage and his belt. Because in between *better* and *all better* there's always some *worse*.

There would be some bad days ahead.

Buckle out days.

In the meantime, Tommy still had the storage room in the back of the school. It had come in handy more than once since that night in the storm. And it wasn't without its comforts. Truman the Custodian was always leaving behind a forgotten bag of chips or a can of soda. Sometimes, it would occur to Tommy that the soda was always cold, or that the chips had been pretty easy to find, and then he'd wonder. Maybe that old custodian wasn't so clueless after all.

Tommy and Winston turned onto a quiet, tree-lined street at the southernmost edge of town. Some of the houses on this block had their porch lights on, and Tommy could see the sign up ahead.

"Almost there," he said.

VANDALS ON THE EDGE OF TOWN

It was the middle of the night and Jack Hought couldn't sleep. So he put the kettle on and sat in his kitchen. And he thought about things.

He lived in a modest but well-cared-for house at the southern-most edge of Cliffs Donnelly, a mere one hundred feet from the city limits between Cliffs Donnelly and the rural county township of South Liberty that bordered it. Of course, ever since he and Stanley Donan had collected the reward for the Holyoke Red Diamond, Jack's friends had been teasing him about taking the money and running. To Florida or Hawaii, somewhere warm and sunny.

And if he was being honest about it, sometimes he was tempted. But he couldn't leave Stanley. And this town was his home, after all.

It was a quiet night, so he could easily hear the two boys pedaling down the street, despite the obvious care they were taking to be silent. They both wore dark hoodies, and the bigger one hauled a duffel bag across his back.

As the boys passed his house, Jack Hought picked up the phone and watched them warily. For a brief moment he thought they might be casing the neighborhood for a car to break into or a house to rob.

But the two riders passed opportunities for each and headed, instead, for the old municipal sign at the city limit. The one welcoming visitors to Cliffs Donnelly.

Jack had been complaining about that darn sign for years, ever since someone had defaced it so that it now read:

if   on ly

But no one ever fixed it.

Upon reaching the sign, the larger boy dropped the duffel bag on the ground and started rooting around inside it. Jack was about to dial 911 when he noticed something. Instead of spray cans, the two boys were taking out stencils and paintbrushes and small bottles of paint.

Jack sat down in the high-back chair by the window and drank his tea as he watched the two boys set to work with a brisk, largely unspoken efficiency. The larger boy painted over the sign entirely, smoothly, carefully, creating a blank slate for the smaller boy, who began reprinting the sign.

Once he was finished, the larger boy took over again, painstakingly working around the edges of the sign with his own paint and brushes. After about twenty minutes, the two boys packed up their supplies and slipped away, back into the night.

After the boys left, Jack Hought drifted off to sleep in his chair.

When he awoke, just before dawn, he put on his robe and some boots and made the one-hundred-foot trek to the sign. As the first rays of sunlight crested over the horizon, he saw that the boys had repainted and restored the sign. But more than that, they had improved it. Though the paint was fresh and new, they had made the sign look old and distressed, weathered but classic. Timeless.

And it now said, in an official, friendly font:

Welcome to Cliffs Donnelly, Ohio
Population: Us

ACKNOWLEDGMENTS

I would like to start off by thanking family, both the one I started and the one that started me. No one does it alone. At least no one I've ever met.

Thank you, Kirsten, the first eyes on anything I write and the first (and often last) voice I listen to.

Thanks to Mom, Dad, and Alison for, among so many other things, allowing me the delusion that I was always the smartest one in the house.

On a more serious note, I am light-years beyond grateful for my editor, Jenne Abramowitz. Thank you for making the book better. Thank you for making me better. Thank you for being our champion.

My thanks to Emily Mitchell, for being my wonderful agent but also for being wonderful before she was my agent. First, by agreeing to read my manuscript despite what I'm sure was one of the least convincing cover letters to pass her desk in some time, and then actually reading that manuscript even though the for-matting of the PDF file had been so corrupted that half the book was crammed into one huge block of text like the longest Latin inscription ever.

This story is, in no small part, about the enduring power (not to mention cumulative effect) of small kindnesses. To this end I would like to thank several people who went out of their way for me, who helped me when they stood to gain nothing for the effort. Who were, simply, kind: Sam Bichara, Gene Reznik, Peter Turchi, Stephanie Mehta, Carolyn Manetti, Bill Straus, Stephen White, Brendan Halpin, Marysue Rucci, Joe Purdy, Donna Rifkind, and Ben Wendell.

Finally, though I've dedicated this book to my teachers, there are two I'd like to single out: Ms. Karen Saupe and Ms. Daryl Yaw. One told me not to fear failure, because it's rarely permanent, and the other advised me that I could stand to close my mouth and listen a bit more because I wasn't nearly as clever as I thought I was.

They were both right.

ABOUT THE AUTHOR

Keith Calabrese is an author and screenwriter who holds a degree in creative writing from Northwestern University. A former script reader, he lives in Los Angeles with his wife, kids, and a dog who thinks he's a mountain goat. This is his first novel.